MISTER JACKS

Mister Jacks is a man naturally more ruthless than his enemies — a condition that serves him well when he agrees to do a favour for his old friend Jacob, the head of a secret anti-terrorist organization. The favour involves escorting a young lady from Kent to Luxembourg who is being targeted by al-Qaeda and al-Hashashin. However, their focus soon shifts to Mister Jacks and they pursue him with a personal vengeance. Now Mister Jacks will need all his ruthlessness to survive. For, if he dies, the young lady dies next. And he would not like such an event to occur.

SPECIAL MESSAGE TO READERS

This book is published under the auspices of

THE ULVERSCROFT FOUNDATION

(registered charity No. 264873 UK)

Established in 1972 to provide funds for research, diagnosis and treatment of eye diseases. Examples of contributions made are: —

A Children's Assessment Unit at Moorfield's Hospital, London.

•

Twin operating theatres at the Western Ophthalmic Hospital, London.

•

A Chair of Ophthalmology at the Royal Australian College of Ophthalmologists.

•

The Ulverscroft Children's Eye Unit at the Great Ormond Street Hospital For Sick Children, London.

You can help further the work of the Foundation by making a donation or leaving a legacy. Every contribution, no matter how small, is received with gratitude. Please write for details to:

THE ULVERSCROFT FOUNDATION,
The Green, Bradgate Road, Anstey,
Leicester LE7 7FU, England.
Telephone: (0116) 236 4325

In Australia write to:
THE ULVERSCROFT FOUNDATION,
c/o The Royal Australian and New Zealand
College of Ophthalmologists,
94-98 Chalmers Street, Surry Hills,
N.S.W. 2010, Australia

Tom Wilson was born in Dumfries, Scotland. His somewhat restless spirit coupled with a need for knowledge led him into a nomadic life that has been richly rewarding by courtesy of those he has met along the way. Tom Wilson currently lives in Somerset, England.

TOM WILSON

MISTER JACKS

Complete and Unabridged

ULVERSCROFT
Leicester

First published in Great Britain in 2007 by
Robert Hale Limited
London

First Large Print Edition
published 2008
by arrangement with
Robert Hale Limited
London

The moral right of the author has been asserted

Copyright © 2007 by Tom Wilson
All rights reserved

British Library CIP Data

Wilson, Tom, *1942 –*
Mister Jacks.—Large print ed.—
Ulverscroft large print series: adventure & suspense
1. Qaida (Organization)—Fiction 2. Terrorism—
Prevention—Fiction 3. Suspense fiction
4. Large type books
I. Title
823.9′2 [F]

ISBN 978–1–84782–369–4

Published by
F. A. Thorpe (Publishing)
Anstey, Leicestershire

Set by Words & Graphics Ltd.
Anstey, Leicestershire
Printed and bound in Great Britain by
T. J. International Ltd., Padstow, Cornwall

This book is printed on acid-free paper

For Jenny

Buckinghamshire Libraries	
and Heritage	
506406	
ULVERSCROFT	26. 2. 10
	16-99

PROLOGUE

The one known as Azrael, had been standing rigid for almost an hour without ever once averting his eyes from the walled villa he was observing. He watched the lights go out one by one and, when the last light went out, the one upstairs in the master bedroom, he smiled into the moonlight.

As a test of his will power, and to give the target time to fall asleep, Azrael stood still for another quarter of an hour. When he finally moved, he moved as a man knowing exactly where he was going and what he was going to do when he got there.

Earlier that afternoon, back in the al-Qaeda safe house in Paris, Azrael studied the floor plans of the house he was about to invade. He knew the layout so well; the challenge had become to reach the target by taking no more than a certain number of steps. He had the figure sixty in his head and it would be interesting later to see how far out he was either way.

On the outside, the villa was guarded by a high wall; on the inside, it was guarded by a supposedly sophisticated alarm system.

Walls were easily climbed and how sophisticated was the alarm system when the main fuse box was situated in the attached garage?

The villa wall was decaying and the cracked rendering offered a multitude of finger and toe-holds. For Azrael, climbing that wall was as easy as walking up a flight of stairs.

Azrael had carefully selected where he would climb the wall. When he dropped down the other side, his appearance was hidden by a huge spreading bush, its spiked leaves rustling in the breeze, and by the shadow of the wall cast by the moon that glowed silver at his back.

A count of ten, listening for any sound that would betray outcry or alarm and then Azrael was off along his elected pathway, hugging the shadowed wall until he stood opposite the double garage attached to the side of the villa. The large door guarding the garage was guaranteed to be as secure as the alarm system but there is neither a lock that cannot be opened nor an electronic system that cannot be breached.

Azrael took a slim, remote-device from an inside pocket of the dark utility jacket he wore and aimed it at the garage door. When he switched it on, a small panel lit up to display a line of four forever changing numbers that came to a stop one by one when the correct code was displayed.

Along with promised security, the garage door also came with a 'run silent, run smooth' claim and when he pressed the button that opened it, he was glad to hear that at least part of the deal had been kept.

He ran towards the opening door; timing his move perfectly, he hit the ground, rolled into the garage while using the remote to close the door behind him. When the door silently settled back into place, he lay a moment bringing his breath back under control. When he was satisfied, he rose to his feet and put on a pair of light intensifying glasses, smiling as around him the darkness was dispelled.

The main fuse-box of the house was on the left side of the garage, set on a wall behind a white Mercedes Benz SL. On reaching the box, Azrael took but thirty seconds to open, then trace and cut the alarm connection.

Alarm disconnected, Azrael moved to the door at the back of the garage that led into the kitchen area. He was prepared to deal with any lock, but Allah smiled on him and he found it already unlocked. Two steps and he was in the kitchen, the door quietly closed behind him.

From there, Azrael started counting his

steps. Eleven steps took him out of the kitchen into a hallway with a mosaic, inlaid floor that was partly covered by a large, multi-coloured rug. Twenty steps took him to the bottom of a wooden staircase; thirty-four took him to the top, every step placed on the outside of each tread for fear of making a familiar creak. Fifty-five took him to the door of the master bedroom, from where he could hear the unsuspecting target snoring. Fifty-seven steps and he was inside the bedroom, back pressed against the closed door, watching the sleeping target as he lay there totally unaware that he had but minutes to live.

Azrael had no time for small calibre handguns. If he was to put a hole in someone then he wanted that hole big enough to guarantee death. He was carrying the gun he always carried, a stainless-steel, six-inch, .357 Magnum Colt Python Elite loaded with mercury-filled, copper-head bullets. Adrenaline racing, he was smiling as he fitted a silencer to the barrel of the especially adapted weapon.

Prepared, Azrael took five steps to the bedside, put the silencer to the sleeping man's right temple and pressed his right hand over the man's mouth, squeezing his nostrils closed with a finger and thumb.

The man's eyes sprang open and, as he struggled, Azrael increased the pressure on his mouth, pressed the silencer tighter against his head and in a soft, cultured English accent, told him to be still. 'When I take my hand away, don't cry out. If you do, your cry will be the last sound you ever hear.'

So saying, Azrael removed his hand and stepped back, the Colt pointed at the man's gaping mouth as he stared wide eyed at the apparition that had suddenly appeared by his bedside.

'Don't say a word,' Azrael warned. 'Just do exactly as I tell you. For a start, sit up, back against the headboard. That's it,' he encouraged as he set the scene. 'Now neatly arrange the pillows around you. Move the one on the left a fraction away from you. That's it. Now sit up straight and clasp your hands across your stomach. Stay like that.'

Azrael played fair and limited himself only to props that were already on scene and, as he came round the bed, he was delighted to see a bowl of fruit resting on a table. Smiling, he took a large green apple from the bowl and held it over the man's mouth. 'Open wide, Wider,' he ordered. When he thought the mouth was open wide enough, he forced the apple into the gaping hole then told the man to bite down hard. 'Harder,' he instructed, as he helped things along by pushing down on the man's head as he pulled him up by the chin, ascertaining that his teeth were firmly embedded in the firm flesh of the apple.

Scene set, Azrael took off the night goggles, laid them on the bedside table, switched on the lamp, and adjusted the shade so as the light was cast across the man's terrified face. Then he went to the bottom of the bed where he stood, pointing the silenced Colt. Rigid with fear, the man was sitting up, clasped hands white-knuckled while his wide eyes expressed as much confusion as dread as he watched the man pointing the gun take a camera-phone from a pocket, adjust the lens, and then point it at him.

'That's it, smile for the camera,' Azrael said encouragingly, as he focused on the man's wide, staring, frightened eyes and began filming. 'I'm going to make you a star . . . Do you remember London, Mr Goldstein?' he went on in a soft voice. 'The house in Golders Green? You should have died there, but you were saved by Mister Jacks, who killed the two sent to kill you. The contract on you has run out. This has nothing to do with al-Hashashin, this has to do with me: this is personal. One of the men Mister Jacks killed was my mentor and as I have hunted you down, so shall I hunt him down,' he concluded, as he shot Goldstein in the face.

The heavy calibre bullet went through the green apple centre shot. When it hit bone, the doctored head exploded, ripping away the base of Goldstein's skull, splattering blood and flesh each side of the headboard.

As Goldstein died, Azrael moved the camera in closer, smiling as he was rewarded with a shot of blood leaking from the bullet hole punched through the apple.

'My codename with the CIA is Hitchcock,' he said, talking to the dead, as he stopped filming and put the camera mobile away inside his jacket. 'But not even the great Tarantino is in my class. It's all fake with Hollywood, fake people, fake guns, fake bullets and fake blood. With me, it's reality all the way,' he went on as he unscrewed the silencer, sliding it away in a pocket made for the job. 'When I shoot a scene, I really shoot it!'

Azrael's bad pun tickled his sense of humour and he had to suppress a giggle as he put away his Colt Python, switched off the bedside lamp, donned his night-goggles and left the room, closing the door quietly on the way out for fear of disturbing the dead.

A few minutes before setting out to kill Goldstein, Azrael had eaten a piece of Afghani Black, that most potent grade of hashish. He had felt the drug working on him during filming and, as he climbed the villa wall, it united with the excitement of the kill, driven on by adrenalin; he was soaring as high as he had ever soared.

By then, the green apple jammed in Goldstein's mouth had long since turned into a red one.

1

Billy Jacks had two mobile phones: the first was open to the few, but the second was open only to one man and when the second one summoned him with a few bars of Tchaikovsky he answered it in the hope that the call would lead to something interesting. Recently the great grey beast boredom had been sneaking up on him and he was suffering a growing need for something to happen that would lead him away from the much too pleasant life of idle luxury he was living. The purchasing power of money had its limits: it could buy imitation danger, but it could not buy the real thing.

And there was nothing like the real thing.

'Hello, Jacob,' Jacks said on answering. 'What can I do for you?'

'I was hoping you might do me a service,' Jacob replied.

'Consider it done,' Jacks responded.

'Without even asking what that service might be?' Jacob questioned.

'If you're asking then you think I'm up for it,' Jacks replied. 'And if you're asking, then it has to involve something dangerous. What more do I need to know? You want I should come and see you?'

'The Norwood house,' Jacob specified. 'And come as soon as you like.'

'I'll be there,' Jacks concluded and it was a different Jacks who terminated the call. Boredom had been swept aside to be replaced with a great sense of expectation. With danger now looming on the horizon, life had taken on a whole new meaning.

With his growing restlessness stilled by anticipation, Jacks took time for a shower, revelling as the hot spray revitalized his body so as to keep it in tune with his now hyperactive mind. As he dressed, he tried to imagine what Jacob might have in mind but it proved a hopeless task. Not that what Jacob had in mind was beyond imagining, but without a clue the variables were as good as infinite.

To Jacks, most people were predictable in thought and in action; Jacob was the exception. You just never knew with him. That was the secret of his success.

All his life, Jacks had been labelled different and in pursuit of a title to hang his difference around he had pursued an on-going inner investigation. One psychologist he visited thought he was a controlled psychopath; another was certain that he had multiple personality disorder, but it was only after visiting an American clinic that he found a condition acceptable to his sensibilities. The clinic specialized in autistic conditions and when, after exhaustive tests, he was diagnosed as having Asperger's Syndrome he found a title he could live with. According to the doctor on his case, his high IQ put him at the top end of the autistic continuum and it had amused him to learn that his difference was all a product of his mind.

Somewhat obsessed with anonymity, Jacks visited each psychologist using an assumed name. He did not mind his researchers knowing all there was to know about a man who did not exist but he balked at them knowing as much about him.

Jack's condition was reflected in many ways. Some reflections showed their face only occasionally; others he lived with permanently. A strong dislike of intrusive noise headed the list; an obsession with neatness that was founded on a love of symmetry came second, so as anxious as he was to learn what Jacob had in mind, he still took time to tidy the apartment so that when he returned to it, he would find the layout pleasing to his eye.

★   ★   ★

Jacks's drive to the Norwood house proved interesting from the observer's point of view. The latest critical terrorist threat on the capital meant a heightening of security and it seemed to him that there were two heavily armed policemen standing at every second set of traffic lights and he did not pass a Tube station without seeing lots of men in black or blue each cradling a Heckler & Koch sub-machine gun. The war on terror was still raging and it was already threatening to rank as the longest war in history, a war that Jacks believed no one was destined to win or to lose. Government security agencies could not lose because it was innocent civilians and not them who were the terrorists' target and, come the end, they could not win the war because how do you defeat an army scattered to the four corners of the globe with each rank and file member ready to die in the name of Allah?

On the other hand, where al-Qaeda could not win in the field simply because they were heavily outnumbered by their civilian targets, they could achieve major victories by way of the fear they could inflict on the people and by the economic chaos they created every time they carried out a terrorist attack or merely threatened to do so.

Religious martyrdom was a mystery to

Jacks. He could not imagine himself giving up his life for any cause other than his own. The very idea of blowing oneself to bits along with who cared how many innocents earning one a passport to Paradise was so illogical, were it not so savage it would be ludicrous. Paradise, like Heaven, was reputed to be a loving peaceful place. Suicide and mass murder was a bizarre price to pay for an entry ticket.

Poor Allah, Jacks thought as he made his way up Norwood Hill, like the Christian God, He must shudder to witness the atrocities committed in His name.

Even sedate Norwood had its share of armed policemen. Jacks had to drive past two wielding Heckler & Kochs and though he barely glanced their way, he knew they would be checking him out with those suspicious eyes that he suspected all policemen were born with. But he was not concerned, even if the police were curious enough to check out the number plate on the Audi, their enquiries would lead them to a name and address in SE London. Jacks was not the man living at that address, but he had a driving licence and documents that said he was.

The Norwood house was situated on a private, tree-lined crescent bordered on each side by similarly grand houses protected by high walls and steel gates. As Jacks made his way round a sweeping bend, the driving window down, he imagined he could smell the wealth that seemed to permeate the air.

Besides noticing just how many policemen were visible on the streets of London, Jacks also noticed that the army of the homeless had grown. Where once a bag lady was a sight to comment upon, on one stretch of street in Crystal Palace, he saw at least half a dozen all wandering aimlessly each oblivious to the other. The present economic recession was biting deeply and it was looking like the old story of the rich getting richer while the poor grew poorer and there could not be many richer than the occupants of the houses he was driving past.

It was a day of observing extremes and Jacks liked that kind of day.

Jacob's residence was guarded by a high wall and the mandatory steel gate that swung open as Jacks approached. There was no coincidence in the gate opening, and from that moment Jacks knew he was being observed by the security cameras that dotted the grounds. Jacks loathed Big Brother and when he parked by the front entrance, he covered his face as he got out of the car. In doing so, he knew he would be bringing a smile to the face of the watching Jacob, but he also knew that Jacob would be expecting no less of him.

The front door opened as Jacks approached and when a hollow voice, transmitted by an internal Tannoy system, invited him into the study — across the hallway, door facing, on the right — he followed the instructions.

As Jacks crossed the entrance hall, behind him the front door by which he had entered sprung the lock closed. The loud click sounded distinctly like the sound of an automatic weapon being primed and Jacks smiled to himself as instinctively he shifted into defence mode.

He did not feel foolish at his reaction; the last time he had heard that sound it was made by a man intent on killing him. The sound betrayed the man priming a .45 automatic and recognizing that sound had saved his life. Had he not reacted so instantaneously, he would now be a long time dead.

With such a memory to respond to, Jacks felt anything but foolish.

2

As Jacks was crossing an expanse of carpet that led to a large oak desk, the door behind him locked automatically. This time, at the sound of the click, he thrust his right hand inside his open jacket, drew an imaginary weapon, spun round while dropping low and ended up pointing an extended finger at the door and saying, 'Bang. Bang. You're dead.'

Jacob chuckled. 'You had to shoot him twice?'

'He was a schizophrenic,' Jacks replied, as Jacob came round the desk to shake his hand.

'Oh, Billy,' Jacob sighed, with a smile and a shake of his head. 'I've met them all, and there is only one of you.'

'And that's good news for all of us,' Jacks responded, as he made himself comfortable on a leather armchair, 'Who needs another me?'

'The CIA,' Jacob suggested. 'But, as it is, I have someone who needs the original you. You will have heard the name Cassandra von Deker?'

'Who hasn't?' Jacks questioned. 'Her picture has been all over the TV and the press. Some serious people tried to take her out.'

'Very serious people,' Jacob stressed. 'What did you make of their attempt?'

'I'd have thought one hitter with a long-gun could have done the job,' Jacks replied. 'As it was, a whole al-Hashashin assassination squad was used. Three cars, three drivers and three hitters. Two took out the driver of the target car and the bodyguard, while the third went after the target. According to the press, he put three bullets through the back window. He couldn't have missed at that range so it had to be that the bullets were deflected by the armoured glass. Whoever the team are, they're cut-and-dried professionals. After the event they disappeared fast. Because they were identified as Arab, and because the target is connected to the arms industry, the law is putting it down as a terrorist operation.'

'Is that how you read the event?' Jacob questioned.

Jacks pulled a face. 'Someone personal could have hired the squad to do the job,' he pointed out. 'But I doubt it. I figure al-Hashashin were doing the job for their parent company, al-Qaeda. What I can't figure, is why they would want to kill a slip of a girl. But you're going to tell me, aren't you?'

'In two days' time, Cassandra von Deker

will be twenty-one.' Jacob replied by way of an answer. 'On that day, she has to present herself at a certain bank in Luxemburg where she will prove her identity by fingerprint before signing the papers that will earn her inheritance. On that day, she will come into a large fortune and, more importantly, she will gain control of Deker Industries. The largest dealer of arms in the world. As well as supplying most of the armies in Europe, their Black Agents also supply any dictator who can pay the bill.'

'Who inherits on her demise?' Jacks asked. 'Is there a brother or sister?'

'There was a brother,' Jacob said informingly. 'A twin brother. Had he lived then, on coming of age, he and Cassandra would jointly have inherited Deker Industries. The brother, Hector von Deker was killed in a plane crash four months ago. Considering that it was a private flight and that eight other people died in the crash no thought then was given to it being an act of murder but with recent events having a voice, it looks like the brother was the target. I now believe that al-Qaeda killed eight innocent people in order to hide their true target while making it look like a terrible accident.'

'So who inherits if the girl is taken out?' Jacks asked.

'If Cassandra doesn't make it to the bank,' Jacob replied, 'then Deker Industries reverts to the board of directors and there are nine of them.'

'Perhaps the decision to kill Cassandra and her brother was a company policy decision,' Jacks suggested drily. 'Who's number one on the board?'

'Rudolf von Siegfried,' Jacob replied. 'He has been with Deker Industries for ever. He's on the way out. My information is that the real voice of the board lies with one Achmid Mudda, a Lebanese naturalized German citizen. He joined the company ten years ago and began as a salesman. With his contacts in the Middle East over the years, he opened up markets in the Lebanon, Iraq, Iran, Syria, Afghanistan and Pakistan. On the surface he was supplying the official armies and security forces of each country, but, inevitably perhaps, a lot of weaponry supplied by him ended up in the hands of al-Qaeda and by way of them into the hands of any terrorist organization worthy of a Kalashnikov.'

'The Kalashnikov,' Jacks echoed with respect. 'The finest long gun ever created. The weapon that won the war in Vietnam. The true weapon of mass destruction. The only difference between it and an atomic bomb is that the bomb kills ten thousand people all at once whereas the Kalashnikov kills as many one by one . . . And you think this Achmid Mudda is al-Qaeda's man in place?

'He's the prime suspect,' Jacob replied. 'I believe al-Qaeda is working towards taking control of Deker Industries and no need to tell you how powerful, how destructive they would become if they controlled a major arms company and no longer needed to buy on the black market.'

'They could have whatever they wanted delivered legally to any port in the world,' Jacks surmised. 'It would take time, but starting with a man they controlled running the board, they would soon have their people planted in all the key positions. Before long they'd be ordering fighter jets and guided missiles. No more need to hijack planes, they'd have the real thing . . . And you want me to deliver Cassandra von Deker safely to the bank?'

'If you wouldn't mind,' Jacob replied. 'There was talk of sending Cassandra to Luxemburg with a posse of armed body-guards, but I think such a move would be so visible as to be dangerous. One man can do the job and no man could do the job better than you.'

'I bet you say that to everyone you want to

do a job for you,' Jacks said, with a knowing smile.

Smiling in return, Jacob replied, 'Only if it's true and it's certainly true in your case. You come at things in your own fashion, Billy, and I would say that a different approach is needed here ... I take it that you're interested?'

Jacks nodded. 'Oh, yes, I'm interested,' he replied. 'Where's the package now?'

Inwardly, Jacob smiled at the thought of how Cassandra von Deker would react to hear herself referred to as a package. 'She's in a safe house in Kent, being guarded round the clock.'

'Whose safe house is it?'

'It's one of mine,' Jacob answered. 'As safe houses go it's as safe as you can get. Those guarding her are men I have used before. The man in charge of security is called Carter. When the time comes, he'll be expecting you.'

'Anyone else in the house?'

'Cassandra's maid, Katrina.'

'I might have known there would be a maid,' Jacks said disapprovingly. 'The rich seem incapable of taking care of themselves. What with their lawyers, their bankers, their solicitors, their accountants, their maids and their butlers, their lives never seem to be in

21

their own hands. Just so long as she doesn't think she's taking her maid with her to Luxemburg. If she does, she's in for a disappointment. It's time she learnt to dress herself.'

'I think Miss von Deker is going to find you somewhat different from the people she is used to,' Jacob said with a smile. 'She's led a somewhat spoiled existence. And that existence has produced a certain coldness. When she was told that her bodyguard/driver of ten years and her personal bodyguard of seven years had been killed, she was rather dismissive of the event.'

'Oh, was she?' Jacks questioned. 'I think I'm going to enjoy meeting this girl. Perhaps I can bring her to see life from a different angle. Tell me where she is and give me the location of the Luxemburg bank then inform your man Carter that I'll be coming to collect her as soon as.'

Jacob gave Jacks the information he requested, secure in the knowledge that he would remember what he had been told. Jacks had the kind of memory that could recall anything it chose to remember. As well as giving Jacks the information requested, Jacob also gave him a false passport and international driving licence for Cassandra to use. 'I presume you have your own.'

'Quite a collection,' Jacks replied. 'I have so many identities in a drawer; I need to be careful that I don't forget who I am.'

Jacob smiled. 'What name shall I give Carter?'

'Tell him Mister Jacks is coming.'

'Mister Jacks,' Jacob echoed 'When al-Qaeda learns, and they will learn, that you are on the case, they'll be sending al-Hashashin after you with a vengeance. Remember the two assassins you killed in Golders Green? Well, poor Mr Goldstein is no longer with us. Two nights ago, in a villa on the outskirts of Paris, he was assassinated by Azrael. He stuck an apple in Goldstein's mouth then shot him through it.'

'And he recorded the killing?' Jacks questioned.

'As ever,' Jacob replied. 'It's being advertised on the website Azrael uses. He's calling Goldstein's death 'the man who said too much' while promising a thrill to chill.'

'I liked Goldstein,' Jacks responded, his face dark. 'He could make me laugh. This Azrael character is a nasty piece of work. I mean, kill them if that's what needs to be done, but don't make a mockery of their death. Azrael is lacking in respect, if I ever bump into him, I'll teach him some.'

'He's al-Hashashin's top man,' Jacob

reminded him as a warning. 'He's on record as having killed seventeen. He once killed three in one day.'

Jacks was not impressed. 'Seventeen sitting targets,' he qualified. 'Nobody shooting back. I'd like to see how he performs if he meets a target who has a gun in his hand.'

'Azrael is known to all the major Intelligence services,' Jacob responded. 'The CIA have codenamed him Hitchcock; we all know that he favours using a Colt Python but, after that, there's not a lot known. Nobody knows what he looks like. And he could be the man they ultimately send after Cassandra von Deker.'

'Let's hope so,' Jacks said sincerely. 'You know me, Jacob. I never get personal, but I do not like this Azrael. I find him offensive in the extreme. I'm all for bodyguarding the ice princess, but there has to be a bit that belongs to me. I'm putting Azrael down as a personal vendetta.'

'I could pity him,' Jacob said, 'but I won't. Al-Hashashin won't give up on Cassandra von Deker. Having missed her once, face and pride are at stake: they'll be honour bound to make the kill. Their intelligence is so good they may already have learned Cassandra's location and they will know she'll need to be moved. But even if they don't have a clue as to where she is now, they know where she needs to be in two days' time. Should you get so far as the bank in Luxemburg, they'll be expecting your arrival. I did say that the mission was dangerous.'

Jacks smiled a somewhat distant smile. 'I wouldn't have it any other way.'

And he meant what he said.

3

On the drive back to his flat, Jacks mused over the al-Qaeda, al-Hashashin partnership. He had never related the structure of al-Qaeda to that of the original al-Hashashin and when he had first learned that the eleventh-century cult had been resurrected and that a modern al-Hashashin was working hand in hand with al-Qaeda, the news had come as somewhat of a revelation.

Hassan Ben Sabbah, the creator of the original al-Hashashin, was a very clever man. He not only turned his trained assassins into a force feared throughout every princedom in the Middle East, he perfected a method of turning innocents into assassins prepared to kill themselves after the event and he did it all by the misuse of the drug, hashish.

When such an assassin was needed, he would send two of his men into a town with instructions to bring a certain kind of man back to the Eagle's Nest, his lair in Mount Lebanon. His agents were looking for a man defeated by life, one reduced to the gutter by the uncaring hand of Fate. Back then, as now, there were many such drunken, homeless men sleeping rough and it never took Ben Sabbah's men long to find the required specimen. When they did, they drugged him and then, when he was unconscious, transported him back to headquarters.

When their hapless victim awoke he found that his rags had turned into the finest silk and that the gutter had turned into a comfortable couch. When he was informed by pretty serving girls that he had died and was now in Paradise how could he doubt their word, why would he ever consider doing so?

Allah was good.

In his time in Paradise, the victim was constantly fed hashish and cannabis derivatives, a diet that kept him in a constant state of ecstasy. With his every whim being catered to, his every desire fulfilled, he quickly became the man Ben Sabbah wanted him to be.

When the time was right, the victim was again drugged to unconsciousness, his silks were removed, his body was dirtied and he was redressed in the rags he had been wearing when found. From there, he was taken from the Eagle's Nest to be returned to the gutter from which he was taken.

From Paradise to the gutter is a great fall and when the man awoke his despair knew no bounds, and the more he proclaimed that he had been to Paradise, the more he was laughed at and mocked.

Ben Sabbah's agents watched the man's progress until one night, wearing black habits and hoods they approached him with an offer he could not refuse. They introduced themselves as the voice of Allah, gave the man a dagger, told him to kill a named target then to kill himself. In doing Allah's will, he would be welcomed back into Paradise.

From where Jacks was sitting, al-Qaeda practised the same device. The victim was no longer a man defeated by life but a young man disillusioned by reality, one trying desperately to hold on to his ideals. The drug used was one much stronger than hashish: it was the drug of religious fanaticism. The victim was no longer given a dagger with which to kill the target and then himself, he was given a bomb to strap to himself and sent out to kill as many innocents as possible while killing himself in the progress.

Different victim, different drug, different weapon, but the process used by al-Qaeda to create killers, runs parallel with the system used by the original Hassan Ben Sabbah. In each case, the reward was the blessing of Allah and guaranteed entry to Paradise.

Jacks found the parallels between al-Hashashin and al-Qaeda intriguing. He had no personal knowledge of religious fanaticism but he did know about hashish. It was the drug on which the hippie generation was weaned and it was hard to grasp that a drug that could encourage people to put flowers down the barrels of soldiers' guns could incite other people to assassination.

Although Jacks had killed men, he had only killed men intent on killing him. He was not like the Hashashin who assassinated anyone for cause or for money. The only cause he followed was the cause of self-defence, and he certainly could not kill anyone for mere money. Perhaps he would never truly define the difference between him and al-Hashashin until the day he was offered money to kill someone he had no personal reason to kill. How he reacted would define his difference, or it would not.

But, until that day dawned, if ever it did, he had the daughter of an arms dealer to see safely to a bank in Luxemburg. As a practising non-capitalist, the great irony of the work he did was that he always ended up protecting capitalists of one variety or another. Most had made their wealth on the backs of the poor, but in Cassandra von Deker's case, the wealth had been acquired from the pockets of the dead. He was curious to meet a woman who had been raised on blood money and to learn how being so raised had affected her personality. The way she had dismissed the deaths of her bodyguards suggested that her upbringing had bred in her a certain self-centred, cold-blooded attitude.

It had been a long time since Jacks had bumped into an ice queen, and he was greatly anticipating meeting Cassandra von Deker.

Had this been a case of a straight delivery of package, when Jacks learned what the package contained, he might possibly have turned down the job, but this was a favour for Jacob. After that, it was one that guaranteed danger and he needed danger like another man needed his pipe and slippers.

In the past, Jacks had protected people whose enemies functioned on limited resources; in the case of Cassandra von Deker and al-Hashashin, he would be dealing with an enemy whose resources were on a par with those of the CIA. Beyond the satellite surveillance and the computer technology, al-Hashashin was a company able to call upon more killers than one.

On passing through the Elephant and Castle, Jacks turned on to the Old Kent Road then drove on to Lewisham where he turned off on to some back streets, eventually parking round the corner from his apartment.

The block he was housed in was secure enough with its electronic system but even so, Jacks checked to see if he'd had any unwelcome visitors since his departure. The talcum powder underneath the front-door mat showed no sign of disturbance and he entered his domain confident that nobody was waiting inside ready to blow his head off. The business he was in bred paranoia, but being a non-paranoid did not rule out having real enemies.

Always check was a rule of the game.

Once inside the flat, he located a holdall which he packed with the necessities and then got down to the serious business of preparing for the mission. Unlocking a cleverly hidden strong box, he retrieved €5000 in large denomination bills, £2000 sterling in smaller bills, two forged passports, one British the other Irish, that came with matching driving licences which he put with the passports and licences prepared for Cassandra von Deker.

Finally, from a drawer in the strong box, Jacks retrieved a .22 Ivor Johnson and laid it handy on a table top. It had been a while since he and Ivor Johnson had kept each other company and it was good to see him again.

Packed for the trip, Jacks took a British atlas from a bookshelf, found the county of

Kent and located the position of the safe house. Next he took down an atlas of Europe, located Luxemburg, and then gave thought on how best to reach his destination.

Britain was an island and there were only three ways to leave it behind; the plane, the ship and the train through the Channel Tunnel. Airports were no place to be if someone was watching out for you. If they missed you before boarding a plane then they were just as likely to be waiting for you when you got off the plane at the other end.

And, besides, the way security had tightened at airports a man would be doing well to smuggle a bottle of water on board a plane far less a firearm.

Ships were death traps; if anything went wrong on board then there was nowhere to run and the security at sea-ports was just as heavy as at airports.

That left the Channel Tunnel and that was looking like the best bet. The car he was planning to use was designed to beat X-ray machines so any weaponry on board would be ninety-five per cent guaranteed to get through. Nothing was ever a hundred per cent safe, the way security systems had advanced, so he would not be surprised to learn of an X-ray machine that could see through lead.

Decision made, he replaced the atlases on the shelf, making sure they were neatly aligned with the other books, straightened an Aubrey Beardsley print that was hanging askew, laid out all he would be taking with him on a low coffee-table then took time out for another shower, revelling in the hot spray that he gradually turned down to as cold as he could stand.

When he got out of the shower he towelled himself dry then dressed for war; a black T-shirt, charcoal-grey easy-fit trousers, a black polo neck cashmere sweater and a pair of boots that had been made for him by an old cobbler in the East End. The soft-soled, black-leather ankle boots looked like any other pair, but underneath the expensive leather they came complete with steel toe-caps, a weapon he had used more than once, and one he had found particularly effective when it came to breaking a man's shin-bone.

Finally, with a certain ceremony, he donned a long, black single-breasted cashmere coat, smiling at his own foolishness as he made sure the euros were safely zipped away in one inside pocket, the passports and licences in another.

Jacks disliked shoulder holsters. His tailored overcoat came with an inside pocket fashioned to hold his Ivor Johnson. When the pistol was firmly in place beneath his buttoned coat, he stood a man prepared for battle. On the surface, he would be fighting someone else's war, but, underneath the surface, way down deep where his heart beat, he would be fighting his own war, one he waged most against himself.

When he left the apartment, he did not leave as Billy Jacks; he left Billy behind and left as Mister Jacks. When it came to fighting a war, Mister Jacks was the man to be.

A few minutes later he was on the way to the safe house in Kent although he doubted if it was anywhere near as safe as Jacob imagined it to be.

In the world of Mister Jacks, nowhere was safe.

4

When Jacks left London behind and moved into Kent, he was feeling as alive as he ever had; there was nothing boosted him more than having a mission to accomplish. As he made his way down yet another lane lined with bare trees, branches reaching beseechingly to the overcast sky, he rang Jacob on the cloned mobile that Jacob had originally supplied. 'All is well?' Jacob asked on answering.

'I'm on my way to the Kent house,' Jacks responded. 'Let Carter know I'll be there within the quarter-hour. Tell him he'll know me by my black, expensive, tailor-made cashmere coat.'

A dry chuckle. 'He'll be very glad to see you.'

'I think I can imagine why,' Jacks responded. 'I bet he'll be glad to get the package off his hands.'

'To put it mildly,' Jacob stated. 'Keep me updated.'

'I will so long as I can,' Jacks qualified, then terminated the call.

When he eventually turned on to the

driveway of the house he wanted, he was not fooled by the open gateway, he knew that somewhere inside the secluded house, someone would be monitoring his progress. But then, he thought, a man couldn't walk up any given High Street in England without the same occurring.

Big Brother knew no boundaries.

As he neared the country house, similar in architecture to any other country house, he spotted two armed guards patrolling the grounds and if he had seen two then he figured that there were at least as many again that he had not seen. With such armament on the outside, he wondered if anyone else inside the house was being kept safe. Jacob said that only Cassandra von Deker and her maid, Katrina, were in residence. But, Jacob was not honour bound to tell him everything he was up to.

Jacks parked the Audi well clear of two 4x4s and, as he got out of the car, he saw a dark-haired man in a grey suit come from the front door to meet him.

'Carter?' he questioned as they shook hands.

'Mister Jacks?' Carter asked in reply.

'That's me,' Jacks confirmed, as Carter led the way through the front door and into a circular hallway that led to a flight of stairs. 'You have a package for me?' he asked, as he took in the man seated at a desk surrounded by monitor-screens and telephones and the two with Uzis patrolling the upper landing.

Carter nodded. 'I hope for your sake you're only delivering her round the corner,' he said lightly.

'She's a headache?' Jacks asked.

'Migraine class,' Carter confirmed. 'She's been treating us like servants since she got here. Earlier today, she asked me if I'd phone Harrods to have them deliver some of her favourite soap, the only one that's compatible with her delicate skin! Can you believe that?'

'People with no real need in their lives can bring meaning to the most meaningless things,' Jacks observed. 'Where is she?'

'South wing,' Carter replied, pointing a finger. 'Turn right top of the stairs, last door you'll meet face to face.'

Jacks followed Carter's directions and when he got to the door, he entered without knocking. He walked into an empty sitting-room and when he went through an inner doorway he walked into the clichéd scene from a thousand movies of madam sitting at a dressing-table having her hair brushed by a maid. Madam saw him coming in the mirror, spun round and said, in the most venomous tone, 'How dare you walk into my bedroom unannounced!'

Jacks ignored her and made straight for the maid. 'Katrina?' he asked of the diminutive girl who nodded in reply.

'How dare you ignore me when I'm addressing you,' Cassandra von Deker interjected.

Again Jacks ignored her as he took Katrina gently by an arm and told her to go to her room. In response, Katrina looked at her mistress for confirmation. 'Never mind looking at her, just do as I say,' Jacks said, holding the girl with a look. The look, put with a certain tone in his voice, had her hurrying out of the bedroom.

'Who do you think you are?' Cassandra wanted to know as she rose angrily to her feet and for a moment Jacks took in the fully made-up face that looked as though it had sucked one too many acid drops.

'I know who I am,' he replied, looking straight into her green eyes. 'It's you who's suffering from delusions. Where's the bathroom?'

Cassandra's angry look was shifted aside by one of confusion. 'The bathroom?' she questioned.

'Don't repeat my questions,' Jacks said firmly. 'Just tell me what I want to know: where's the bathroom?'

'That door,' Cassandra replied, raising a

slim hand, pointing an elegant finger.

'Lead on,' Jacks invited, and when Cassandra stood still he took her by an arm and led her across the floor, as good as pushing her into the bathroom before locking the door behind them.

'Are you mad?' Cassandra asked.

'Possibly,' Jacks said, as he turned on the two bath taps and the two in the sink, each one running at a different volume than the other. 'You'll have seen this in the movies,' he said, as he stood close to the woman, towering over her, looking down into her eyes. 'Spies use this device if they suspect the place is bugged, and, as this is a safe house run by a friend of mine, then it's definitely bugged. Loud music doesn't work, it's too easy to separate the sounds, but four running taps beats them every time. Your maid first. Tell me about her.'

'My maid?' Cassandra questioned.

'You're doing it again,' Jacks said disapprovingly. 'Just tell me about Katrina. How long has she been with you?'

'About five months.'

'What happened to the one before?'

'Her parents won big on the Italian lottery and they sent her tickets to come home.'

Oh, did they, Jacks thought. 'And where did you find the Moroccan girl?'

'Marie, my first maid, introduced her. They were friends at college. Studying English together.'

Convenient, Jacks thought. 'Right,' he stated. 'Listen to me and listen carefully, then do exactly as I say,' he continued, in a forceful whisper, taking Cassandra by her upper arms and pulling her closer, inhaling an overdose of expensive perfume as he did so. 'First thing,' he went on, 'the way you look, at every set of traffic lights we pull up, someone on the pavement will be pointing a finger at you and shouting your name. For a start, wash your mask off your face, tie up your hair and get rid of all this,' he continued, flicking a diamond-drop ear-ring and the gold heart that hung at her throat. 'And the fortune you're wearing on your fingers.'

'Not my locket,' she asked, in a subdued voice as she clutched the gold heart in a pale hand. 'It means so much to me.'

'Then cover it up,' Jacks instructed. 'But get rid of the rest. When you're finished in here pack a small suitcase, just the essentials, anything we need we'll buy along the way. Don't bring any mobile phones along . . . '

'They've already confiscated my phones,' Cassandra said, with a hint of sulkiness,

'I'm glad to hear that,' Jack said. 'If you're being hunted, then carrying an undoctored mobile around is like wearing a flashing neon sign on your head that says 'Here I am, come and get me'. The same goes if you use a credit card, so leave all yours behind. After that, get out of that expensive dress you're wearing and into a pair of jeans and a short, warm coat. Avoid the mink. I know it won't be easy for you, but I need you to look ordinary. The less you look like yourself, the safer you will be.'

'I couldn't look ordinary even if I tried,' Cassandra claimed.

'Just do your best,' Jacks advised. 'It may surprise you what you'll find under the face you wear for the world . . . Fifteen minutes and I'll be back. Then we get out of here.'

'You're the man taking me to Luxemburg?' Cassandra asked with a hint of alarm.

'It's your lucky day,' Jacks replied.

So saying, he turned off the taps and left the bathroom, leaving behind a much confused Cassandra von Deker. It was not so much that the man with the penetrating dark eyes had verbally abused her, but her confusion that she had stood still and allowed him to do so. No man, not even her father, had ever spoken down to her like that, she thought, as she began removing the make-up from her face. But the man with the penetrating eyes was right, the way her

41

picture had been all over the news, she could not go very far without someone recognizing her and anyone who did so could be out to kill her. She had different theories about who wanted her dead, but whoever was behind the assault on the car in Kensington had sent six men to kill her. Whoever they were, they were serious in their intent. With the prize being Deker Industries, she suspected the entire company board. Each of them would benefit from her not reaching Luxemburg; any one of them could be behind things, or all of them.

She often missed her brother; at a time like this she missed him even more. He was weaker than she was but he'd had an understanding of her that was unique to him.

She had never been alone when she was with Hector.

★　★　★

When Jacks left the bathroom, he went to the maid's room where he found her sitting on a bed, staring out of a window. The scene painted a forlorn picture and he wondered if Katrina had created it for him to see.

'Come downstairs with me a moment,' he instructed, holding open the bedroom door.

Katrina immediately rose to her feet and approached in a timid manner that Jacks thought she might be faking, but as she passed him in the doorway, he smelt fear on her and he wondered if it was simply a product of her supposed timidity, or if it was fear born much deeper, a fear of giving herself away?

From there, Jacks took Katrina downstairs where he found Carter waiting with a questioning look on his face. 'Everything all right?' Carter asked.

'Couldn't be better,' Jacks answered. 'I wonder, is there somewhere Katrina could get a hot drink? The girl's had a trying few days.'

Carter understood and called one of the guards over, instructing him to take Katrina to the staff-room and supply her with a hot beverage. As Katrina was docilely led away, Jacks watched her departure and where her look showed no sign of alarm, her tightened body language betrayed a heightening of her fear.

'A problem?' Carter asked.

'I presume you did a background on the maid,' Jacks said, by way of reply.

'All the way back,' Carter replied. 'She came out squeaky clean.'

'And the previous maid?' Jacks questioned. 'Did her parents really win the lottery?'

'A cheque for a million euros, authorized

by a lottery company, was deposited in their joint bank account around five months ago,' Carter said informingly, a hint of a smile hovering around his lips. 'You think someone might have paid a million just to get Katrina a job as a maid? Why not just buy Marie direct? It's a lot of money just to arrange a plant.'

'It's small change when it gets to Deker Industries being the reward,' Jacks pointed out. 'And perhaps they figured Marie so loyal to the Deker woman she was unbuyable. So they bought her out of the job instead.'

'And then arranged for her to hand the job over to Katrina?' Carter asked, now smiling openly.

'No,' Jacks corrected. 'If my suspicions are in any way correct, then Katrina arranged that part herself. Marie might have thought she was doing Katrina a favour but, if I'm right, she was manipulated into doing so. How hard can it be to manipulate the mind of a maid?'

Carter shook his head. 'I've met my share of suspicious minds, I have one myself, but yours is way ahead. Paranoia is just round the corner: best watch your step.'

It was Jacks's turn to smile. 'I was being driven by a man once,' he said, looking Carter directly in the face. 'When all of a sudden, he changed gear, and took off at high speed, ignoring a red light in the process. He kept this up for five or ten minutes, eventually turning into a coal yard in New Cross where we came to a stop behind a slagheap.

'"What was that all about?' I ask.

'"Didn't you see the green van?' he asks in reply. 'It was following us.'

'"You can't be sure it was following us,' says I.

'"You're right,' he agrees, 'but I can be sure now that it isn't.''

Carter smiled. 'I'll pass that one on. Was the driver in the business?'

'No,' Jacks replied. 'He's smarter than us; he robs banks for a living. Whatever you think of me, do me a service and keep Katrina in the staff-room until the woman and me are clear of the house.'

'Consider it done,' Carter replied. 'You're leaving soon?'

'As soon as,' Jacks replied, as he turned away and made for the stairs.

★   ★   ★

This time, Jacks entered the sitting-room unannounced, but he knocked on the bedroom door. When he was invited to come in he found Cassandra von Deker, a canvas sling-bag in her hand, standing by a closed

45

suitcase over which was folded a short suede jacket. 'Excuse me,' he said with a smile, as he took in her oval face wearing a minimum of make-up and her long hair now twisted up, secured by a tortoiseshell comb. 'Have you seen Cassandra von Deker? I was supposed to meet her here.'

Almost against her will, Cassandra smiled. 'I look that different?'

'Completely,' Jacks qualified. 'And you were right: you couldn't look ordinary if you tried. With those big green eyes of yours, and that mouth, you're a very pretty girl.'

Cassandra did not quite bristle, but her voice was short when she said, 'I may look like a girl but I begin by being a woman.'

Jacks smiled. 'I'll take your word for that,' he responded, as he handed her the suede jacket and picked up her suitcase. 'Now, let's get out of here, safe houses give me the creeps.'

As she followed Jacks out of the suite and down the stairs, she wondered about a man who one moment came on like a tiger shark and the next could express himself like a child.

Perhaps the real man lived somewhere in between.

5

As Jacks pulled away from the Kent house, he told Cassandra to put on her seat belt.

'Safety first?' she questioned as she did as asked.

'It's against the law in the UK to travel in a car without wearing a seat-belt,' Jacks explained. 'And I don't want two bored policemen pulling us over for a lecture. Besides, the way I drive you'll probably need it.'

When Jacks left the leafy lanes behind and hit a stretch of open road, he caught his breath then let it out as a long sigh.

'Are you all right?' Cassandra asked, with a hint of concern.

'Oh, yes,' Jacks confirmed. 'I'm all right.'

'That was a strange sigh,' she observed. 'It sounded like it came from the bottom of your heart.'

Jacks smiled just for her and asked, 'Who says I've got a heart? If I find out who's spreading these malicious rumours about me, I'll be tracking them down.'

Cassandra smiled in response. 'You're the first bodyguard I've met who has a sense of humour.'

'You're assuming that I'm joking,' Jacks said, this time keeping his smile to himself. 'A man with a heart couldn't have done some of the things I've needed to do.'

Outside of asking the obvious question, Cassandra could find nothing to say in response to Jacks's statement. She did not ask perhaps because she did not want to pry, or perhaps because she did not want to hear the answer to her question.

Either way, she said nothing as she lapsed into a thoughtful silence.

Cassandra was wearing an expensive musk perfume and, as its sweet odour invaded the atmosphere inside the car, stimulating his senses, Jacks opened a window and invited in the fresh air. A few deep breaths, the wind on his face and he contacted Jacob on the cloned mobile. 'We've not long left the house,' he said on receiving a reply. '*En route* to the garage,' he concluded, terminating the call.

'The garage?' Cassandra questioned.

'You'll see when we get there,' Jacks replied, as he again checked his rear-view mirror. 'There doesn't appear to be anyone following us.'

'You sound disappointed,' Cassandra observed.

'Wrong word,' Jacks answered, as he hit a stretch of clearway and overtook a line of cars, the sudden thrust of the engine causing

Cassandra to be pulled back in her seat. 'I'm not disappointed, I'm surprised, and my surprise is giving me cause for concern.'

'Surely it's good news,' Cassandra said naïvely.

'It could be,' Jacks responded, 'but I doubt if it is. The people on your case are highly organized. Up there with the CIA. We have to assume that they know where you've been since they missed you in Kensington and if they know that much, then they know that you've recently left. Which means they have to be following us one way or the other.'

'What other way is there?' Cassandra asked.

'Satellite surveillance,' Jacks replied, his mind turning over the possibilities. 'And if they're on to us via satellite, then chances are we have a tracking device on board. Either planted on the car, on you, or on me.'

'How can we find out?' Cassandra asked in alarm.

'We can't find out now,' Jacks observed. 'We could spend forever taking this car apart. But we will find out within half an hour after we get to where we are going.'

'How do you know that?' Cassandra questioned.

'I know that because if we are being tracked by satellite, then the people following us are a couple of miles behind, watching our progress on a laptop computer,' Jacks explained. 'Once we stop at our destination, it'll take them ten minutes to catch us up and then another ten minutes or so to organize the hit. If nobody shows up within that time, then we can assume we're clean.'

'What do we do if the killers do turn up?' Cassandra asked, somewhat surprised at how calmly she was taking this turn of events.

'You do exactly as I tell you to do,' Jacks replied, giving Cassandra a direct look. 'And I'll do the rest.'

Cassandra nodded. 'Can I ask who you work for? The person you just phoned?'

'I don't work for anybody: I'm freelance,' Jacks said. 'The man I'm doing this one for ends by running some secret government agency, but he begins by being a long-time friend of mine. Some time back, I was being hunted by a killer. Without my friend's help, I probably would have lost the war.'

'But you didn't,' Cassandra stated.

'No, I won it,' Jacks said, smiling at a distant memory. 'And ever since then my friend has involved me in all kinds of interesting situations. He can cater to my needs.'

As Cassandra wondered what those needs might be, she asked, 'What do they call you?

You know my name, secret or not, it's only fair that I know yours.'

Jacks smiled in reply. 'I don't really understand being fair,' he commented. 'But they call me Mister Jacks.'

'I can't call you 'mister' all the way to Luxemburg,' Cassandra said shortly.

'Then don't call me anything,' Jacks suggested. 'Bearing in mind that by any name a rose is just as thorny.'

Cassandra did not recognize the quote. 'Who said that?' she asked.

'I did,' Jacks replied. 'I like to lift the odd line from a movie. But mostly, I like to say it for myself.'

Stranger and stranger, Cassandra thought as she tried yet again to evaluate the man driving her through the countryside.

The man who almost certainly held her life in his hands.

★　★　★

The garage, as it was known, was a secure unit situated on an industrial estate in Catford, SE London. On paper, the unit was rented by a construction company; in reality it was the property of Jacob's organization, and the only construction done there involved vehicles and weapons. The place came complete with sleeping-quarters which made it a handy location in which to hole up.

When Jacks turned on to the industrial estate darkness was falling and he welcomed it as a friend, but then, he had always felt more at home under a midnight moon rather than under a noonday sun.

When he pulled up at the door of the unit he wanted, he retrieved a slim remote from under the driving seat and aimed it at the shuttered door. A faint click and the door slowly rose open. As soon as it was high enough, headlights on, he drove into the garage, parked, leaving the engine running, then quickly closed the door behind him.

'Get out of the car,' he said, as he did the same, going quickly to the shuttered door that he secured at the bottom by three clamps set in the concrete floor. Then he switched on some lights, illuminating one side of the unit while leaving the other side cast in shadows. The lights revealed a line of vehicles parked beside a machine shop boasting a lathe and sundry cutting machines and after switching off the Audi engine, he made directly for a dark-blue Ford Focus with the keys in the boot-lock. As he raised the boot, Cassandra joined him, watching fascinated as he opened a lead-lined compartment, revealing an array of handguns, silencers and ammunition.

'Take this,' he instructed, handing Cassandra a .45 automatic. Rather hesitantly, she accepted the weapon, watching wide-eyed as Jacks fitted a silencer to his adapted Ivor Johnson. 'You ever fired a gun?' he asked, as he went to a table bearing two security screens and switched them on.

'Only a shotgun,' Cassandra replied, in a somewhat hoarse whisper. 'Clay pigeons,' she explained, the reality of her situation drying her mouth as it flooded her system with adrenaline-charged fear.

'It's a start,' Jacks responded, as the screens flickered to life. The front and back of the unit were covered by a fish-eye lens. One screen depicted the outside road and units opposite, the other depicted the rear yard enclosed by a brick wall.

'They'll need to come in by the back door,' Jacks said softly, his eyes focused on the screen depicting the front. 'I've secured the front.'

'Do you really think someone will come?' Cassandra asked.

'If they do,' Jacks replied, 'there'll be more than one . . . and this looks like them now . . . ' he tailed off as a screen showed a black BMW glide by then turn into the side of a unit opposite. 'Three men. Probably the same team that missed you in Kensington,' he said, taking Cassandra by an arm and leading her to and up a set of metal stairs that led to a wooden door. 'In here,' he instructed, opening the door. 'Lie on the floor, facing the stair head. That's it,' he went on encouragingly. 'Now hold the gun in both hands and aim it at the top stair. If anyone's head but mine appears then blow it off. But don't worry; you'll only need to do this if I'm dead. And I'm not an easy man to kill.'

So saying, Jacks left Cassandra and went back downstairs, switched on an overhead fan and the lathe then passed through a door to the left of the stairs that led into the rear section of the unit.

Leaving the door ajar, letting in a strip of light, he went to the far right-hand corner where he positioned himself behind a stack of cardboard boxes. The rear entrance was in the left-hand corner and his eyes never left it for a second, standing stock still in the darkness like a pillar of ice, adrenaline racing as he anticipated what was going to happen next.

One minute, two minutes, the seconds slithering by like snakes, Jacks stood there until a definite click he heard above the noise being made by the lathe told him the back-door lock had been sprung. Back pressed tight against the wall, he watched as three figures entered the unit, fanning out as they approached the ribbon of light that drew them as the flame drew the moth.

As the three stealthily moving figures approached the door leading into the front of the unit they converged and, picking his moment, Ivor Johnson raised, Jacks stepped out of the shadows and said, 'Pssst!'

All three men were carrying a silenced gun in their right hand. The one on the outside left reacted first, coming round the short way in a quarter arc and Jacks shot him in the right temple. Outside right made the mistake of coming round the long way, a three-quarter arc, and Jacks shot him in the forehead. The one in the centre froze and, as he approached him, Jacks said, 'You either go for it or I back-shoot you.' In response, the man dropped his weapon and raised his hands in the air. 'I did warn you,' Jacks said, as he shot him in the back of the head.

An Ivor Johnson is a .22 calibre marksman's pistol but the bullets in Jacks's gun had been doctored with dum-dum explosive points and where they had left a small entry wound on the way in, on the way out they had essentially blown the three heads apart, splattering brains, flesh and blood across the unit wall.

Jacks relocked the rear door, checked the three pulses, ascertaining that the three men were dead then he searched them, finding only a small remote connected to a BMW key that he put in a pocket. Finally, he collected the three dropped guns, noting that they were identical Heckler & Koch USP9s, and carried them into the front part of the unit, closing the door behind him on the thought that there was no need for Cassandra to see the bodies.

When he had deposited the H & Ks on a table, he made for the stairs while calling out to Cassandra that she was safe now. On reaching the top stair, he was a little surprised to find her still lying on the floor.

'You can get up now,' he said.

'No I can't,' Cassandra replied, looking everywhere but up at Jacks. 'I'm too embarrassed. I've had a bit of an accident.'

Jacks understood and, as he knelt, taking the .45 from a pale hand, and putting it into her canvas bag, he told her not to worry about it. 'There's a shower in the back, towels, all you will need. You do what you have to do and I'll bring your suitcase up. I'll leave it outside the door.'

'God, I feel so ashamed,' Cassandra almost cried.

'There's no need,' Jacks said consolingly, as he turned for the stairs. 'Fear can play tricks on the body.'

By the time Jacks carried the suitcase upstairs, Cassandra was already under the shower and he smiled sympathetically before going back downstairs where he moved his holdall from the Audi into the boot of the Ford Focus. While there, he reloaded his Ivor Johnson, unscrewed the silencer, replaced it in the lead-lined compartment and sealed it closed. As he did so he reviewed the fact that he had just killed three men.

Jacks felt no qualms about having done so, no twinge of conscience. The men were out to kill Cassandra and himself; they deserved to die. Admittedly, he had shot an unarmed man in the back of the head, but had he not then that man may have lived on to kill again. It was doubtful if anyone else would be so forgiving and understanding of his actions, but he practised a philosophy of if it was all right with him, then it was all right with him.

And in this case, it was perfectly all right.

6

There was an electric kettle on site and when Cassandra, looking rather sheepish, came back downstairs, suitcase in hand, Jacks gave her a cup of strong black coffee. 'Take a couple of mouthfuls of this,' he said. 'And don't worry about a thing.'

'I don't know what came over me,' she said defensively, as she accepted the coffee. 'I didn't do anything so foolish when they tried to kill me in Kensington.'

'What came over you was fear,' Jacks explained, as he lifted her suitcase and put it in the boot of the Focus. 'Kensington was different from tonight. In Kensington it was over before you knew it. Tonight you were waiting with a gun in your hand in case you needed to kill someone. In Kensington, any fear you had came after the event, tonight, fear was working on you from the start. But I don't want to hear any more about it. As far as I'm concerned it was just one of those things ... Now, drink up, we need to get out of here but, before we do, there's a small matter of a tracking-device that needs to be resolved.'

'You know where it is?' Cassandra questioned, then drained her coffee cup.

'I think so,' Jacks claimed. 'I don't think it's on the Audi. I'm pretty certain no one got close enough to plant it on me. That leaves you.'

'Where?' Cassandra asked. 'In my suitcase?'

Jacks shook his head. 'Highly unlikely,' he said. 'If you plant a tracking device on somebody you have to make certain that you plant it on something they're guaranteed to always have on their person. A suitcase you might abandon, clothes you may change or leave behind. A purse or wallet is good, but as you carry neither what are we left with? What's the one thing you always carry or, in this case, always wear around your neck?'

'My locket,' Cassandra exclaimed, as in response to Jacks's outstretched hand she took it from round her neck, watching intrigued as he opened it to reveal two pictures, one of her brother and one of herself. Using a pair of electrician's tweezers, he raised the picture of Cassandra to reveal nothing, then the picture of her brother to reveal a small square of what looked like metal gauze. 'There you go,' Jacks said, as he removed it and handed the locket back to Cassandra.

'Who put it there?' Cassandra asked, as she

replaced the locket around her neck.

'My money's on your maid Katrina,' Jacks replied. 'I bet you take off your locket when you take a shower and where do you put it when you do?'

'On my dressing-table,' Cassandra said, as realization flooded her face.

As they were talking, more than once, Jacks saw Cassandra's eyes drift towards the door that led into the rear of the unit. When they drifted there yet again, he said, 'You have nothing to worry about. The men who came to kill you are all dead.'

'You killed all three?' Cassandra asked in a quiet voice.

'They died of heart failure,' Jacks replied. 'But it was me that stopped their hearts.'

'You killed three men so I could go on living,' Cassandra stated, as she gave Jacks an open, adoring look.

'Only secondly,' Jacks qualified. 'First, I killed them so as *I* could go on living. I might be fighting under your colours, but it's my battle. Now, let's get out of here,' he concluded, leading the way to the Focus where he held open the passenger door.

'We're travelling in this?' Cassandra asked, with a hint of a smile.

'Don't be fooled by the domestic appearance,' Jacks said, smiling in turn. 'It's a

Ferrari in disguise,' he claimed, before going to the entrance door, releasing the clamps that held it firmly embedded in the concrete floor and then rejoined Cassandra in the car.

When Jacks was out of the garage, door secured behind him, he pulled alongside the parked BMW and got out of the Focus. Using the key he had found on one of the killers, he opened the BMW and checked the inside where he discovered a laptop and a switched-off mobile phone. Leaving them where they were, he relocked the car and put the keys behind a front wheel.

When he was free of the industrial estate, Cassandra sitting quiet and thoughtful beside him, Jacks contacted Jacob on the cloned mobile. The call was answered quickly and he detected a concerned note in Jacob's voice when he asked if all was well.

'A bit messy,' Jacks replied. 'I'm afraid you'll need to send in the cleaners. There's three big bags of rubbish in the back of the garage need shifting.'

'Three?'

'They were amateurs,' Jacks claimed. 'I've left their H and Ks on a table; check out the numbers for me and see if you can trace them to source. And there's a black BMW parked across the way, keys on the front wheel. The car probably won't tell you much, but inside you'll find a laptop and a mobile phone. From them, you should learn much. Like I said, they were amateurs.'

'You have been busy,' Jacob said respectfully. 'How is Cassandra?'

'She's safe. A bit shook up perhaps but she's a brave girl,' Jacks replied, giving Cassandra an encouraging smile. 'Get in touch with Carter. Tell him the maid is wrong. She planted a tracking device on the package and who knows how much information she's passed on in between. If the other people didn't know before then it's pretty certain that they now know I'm on the case and I don't think they'll be too happy with me.'

'I suspect you are correct there.' Jacob agreed. 'Where now? It's getting late.'

'Harry's,' Jacks replied. 'Let him know I'm coming and tell him to sort out the biggest fillet steak he can find — all the trimmings. I've a lot of thinking to do and I need first to stop thinking about food.'

'All will be done,' Jacob stated, and Jacks sensed that he was smiling as he spoke.

'Tell Harry not to forget the mushrooms,' Jacks responded then terminated the call.

'You can think about food at a time like this?' Cassandra asked respectfully.

'If I stopped thinking about food at a time

like this, I'd have starved to death long ago,' Jacks replied. 'Most of my life has been times like this.'

Yet again Cassandra was at a loss for words.

Jacks followed the Old Kent Road into London, a route that took him almost past the block of flats he lived in, but he gave no thought to home. Home was where Billy lived and, come the end, it would be good to see him again but, for now, he was Mister Jacks and Mister Jacks had a job to do.

Just before the Elephant and Castle, Jacks pulled into a petrol station, parking behind a behemoth of a lorry. When he had filled the Focus, on the way to pay the bill, he appeared to drop something and when he bent to pick that something up, he planted the tracking device inside a rear mudguard of the lorry. The legend on the side of the lorry declared that it was the property of a Scottish company and Jacks hoped it was being driven all the way to John O'Groats.

Job done, bill paid, Jacks joined Cassandra and drove off feeling a contented if somewhat hungry man.

He had won the opening encounter; now all he had to do was win the battle.

★ ★ ★

The detached house on the outskirts of Watford looked little different than any other house on the private estate. It sat in its own grounds, it had a wall around it and three cars parked outside from nine to five were of the family variety. Like many such houses, this one had been converted into office premises and three brass plaques by the front door, each one polished smooth over time, declared who occupied the space. The top plaque advertised an accountant, the middle one a financial consultant and the bottom one an investment broker, but where it appeared that neither was connected to the other, the three were in fact a tightly knit trio who worked for the same solitary client.

Above ground level, the house looked the same as a thousand others, but, beneath the mask of normality, housed in a specially constructed, extended basement, it was a world of high-tech surveillance and intelligence gathering that was the British headquarters of al-Qaeda.

At present three men were on duty in the basement, Rimmon, al-Hashashin's top man in England, the one running the Cassandra von Deker operation and Omar and Achmir the computer experts. Between them, Omar and Achmir claimed to be the best hackers on the planet; there was not a firewall they could not breach, nor a computer code they could not crack and, in all their years of serving al-Qaeda, their claim had yet to be proved false.

The basement was always a busy, atmospheric place but, tonight, there was an unfamiliar sense of urgency in the air as a rare sense of defeat pervaded the atmosphere.

Over the last hour or so, Rimmon, a man known for his calm, had evolved into a hyperactive, agitated machine fond of raising its voice. 'Where is he now?' he questioned angrily.

'North London,' Achmir replied, his eyes fixed on a computer monitor. 'He appears to be making for the M1 motorway.'

'The M1?' Rimmon echoed, with a puzzled shake of his head. 'He's supposed to be making for Luxemburg! Something has gone terribly wrong,' he decided. 'If Jacks is on the move then whatever happened on the industrial estate is long over and done with. I can't reach our people. As things stand, we have to assume that they are dead and that they were killed by Mister Jacks.'

'All three?' Omar questioned doubtfully.

'They are from your best,' Achmir reminded.

'A bullet kills the best as fast as it does the worst,' Rimmon pointed out. 'Bullets and the nerve is all it takes and I'm sure Mister

Jacks has plenty of each. Not long ago, he killed two of our men in Golders Green and one of those men was Azrael's mentor, Azrael is going to be unpleased when he learns that again we have lost to Jacks . . . It can't be him that we're tracking,' he continued, in a thoughtful tone. 'When our people turned up on the industrial estate, Jacks knew they didn't get there by chance. He's too good to have been followed by car so he must have worked out that he had a tracking device on board. And if he thought it, then he found it, and when he did, it didn't take him five seconds to know who had planted it. Since then he's planted it on another vehicle heading in the opposite direction. Contact Katrina, tell her to get out of there and to contact us when she is clear.'

In response, Omar ran his fingers over a keyboard and after four attempts, informed Rimmon that Katrina could not be reached: her mobile was dead.

Rimmon nodded resignedly. 'The laptop our people were using to follow Jacks — can you get into it and burn everything?'

'Consider it done,' Achmir responded, as he set his fingertips dancing over a keyboard. 'But don't worry, no one could trace us. The route is encrypted then bounced round the world. Anyone trying to crack it needs only to take one wrong turn and the whole system is programmed to crash.'

Rimmon was relieved. It was turning out to be a very bad night and where Mister Jacks had caused the disaster it was the man he was working for who was ultimately responsible. The one who called himself Jacob; the one the CIA codenamed the Fox but who was known to al-Qaeda and al-Hashashin as the Jew. The British Government and MI5 might imagine that the Jew served them, but the only country he had ever served was Israel and the secret service he served best was the one known as MOSSAD.

The Jew was an enemy of old and so far he was winning their latest encounter. His man in the field, Mister Jacks, was on the loose somewhere and Rimmon knew he had best find him quickly. When he reported in tonight's failure, after the mistakes in Kensington, he would be marked down as a two-time loser; to lose a third time would probably cost him his life. It would not do to wait until Mister Jacks reached Luxemburg and then have him killed by Azrael. If he was to redeem himself in the eyes of those he served then he would need to get to Jacks before he reached his final destination.

As Rimmon considered what next to do, he

realized that, for him, the focus of the hunt had shifted. The von Deker woman was still the ultimate target but Mister Jacks had become number one priority.

Rimmon wanted to see him dead.

7

Harry's place was situated on a square in Ladbroke Grove, West London. Built during the Victorian era, it no doubt began life as a fashionable hotel for a gentleman to take his mistress on a wet Sunday afternoon but, as the years had not been kind to the neighbourhood, neither had they been kind to the hotel. During its evolution the hotel had been reduced to a bed and breakfast establishment, a brothel that catered to those of bizarre inclinations, an illegal gambling club run by the local Mafia and finally a crack-den run by some posse or other. After the den was closed by the police the property fell into a state of decay and would no doubt have been destined for demolition had not Jacob learned of its existence and realized its potential.

Once purchased, a horde of builders and architects descended on the Ladbroke Grove property and they began by knocking out half the ground floor to create a way into the large back garden that they concreted to turn into a secure parking area. When the inside of the property was refurbished and easy access round the back was no longer needed, the entrance to the car-park was sealed by a steel shutter that had evolved into the kind that opened and closed electronically. What made this shutter door different was that it could only be opened or closed from inside the premises and Jacks smiled as it opened before him then closed behind him, leaving him locked in what he rated as the safest safe house in the world.

'You'll like Harry,' Jacks said, as he got out of the Focus, taking his Ivor Johnson with him. 'He's a man of few words.'

'It would make a nice change to meet someone likeable,' Cassandra said, as she joined Jacks at the rear of the car and they retrieved their luggage from the boot.

'Now I'm hurt,' Jacks said jokingly, laying a hand on where he thought his heart might be.

Cassandra flushed. 'I wasn't referring to you,' she said defensively. 'I was referring to all these hateful people who are trying to kill me.'

'I know,' Jacks responded, as he led the way to a rear entrance. 'And those same people are now truly intent on killing me. I cost them three men tonight; it wouldn't surprise me if they wanted me now even more badly than they want you. So we'd best take care,

Cassandra. I watch your back, you watch mine . . . OK?'

As Jacks asked the question, he gave Cassandra such an intense look that she felt the heat from his eyes cascade throughout her entire system. Not trusting her voice, she nodded while giving Jacks a look that she hoped was just as intense.

Whatever Jacks read in her look, seeing it caused him to smile and Cassandra was only saved from total confusion as the back door opened and a friendly voice invited them to come in.

Jacks and Cassandra followed Harry through a second door that led out into a spacious, discreetly lit hallway. 'It's good seeing you again,' Harry said softly, as he retrieved two keys from a cubby-hole office and handed one to Jacks, the other to Cassandra, 'Rooms three and five. Upstairs, right, end of the corridor. I'd even heard that you were dead.'

'I was,' Jacks quipped as he accepted the key. 'I came back to haunt a few.'

Harry almost smiled. 'Dinner in an hour. Usual place.'

'Mushrooms and all?' Jacks questioned, as he turned for the stairs.

'As requested,' Harry replied.

As Cassandra and Jacks walked along the

upstairs corridor, she commented on how right he had been to describe his friend as a man of few words.

'He's not my friend,' Jacks corrected. 'He's a man I like when we meet, but in between I never spare him a thought. Did you notice that he never addressed me by any name and where he almost certainly knew who you were, he never betrayed the knowledge, never batted an eye,' he concluded respectfully as they reached their rooms. 'That one's yours,' Jacks said. 'I'll give you a knock when the time comes.'

'Shall I dress for dinner?' Cassandra asked.

Jacks smiled his first free smile of the day. 'You're a case, aren't you?' he asked quite gently. 'Here we are hiding out in a house of mystery while being hunted by assassins intent on killing us and you're wondering if you should dress for dinner! You're a wonder, that's what you are! Different worlds, kid. Different worlds,' he concluded, before entering his room, leaving Cassandra watching the door being closed on her, standing there feeling very foolish indeed while not understanding why she should feel so.

Surely everyone dressed for dinner?

Once inside his allocated room, Jacks dropped his hold-all, locked the door with a hand behind his back, leant against it and let loose a breath he seemed to have been holding all day. There were security cameras on the outside of the safe house but there were none on the inside and for the first time that day, he felt free of prying eyes. He did not imagine that people were watching him, he knew for a fact that they were. CCTV cameras watched him on his journey to Jacob's Hampstead house; Jacob watched him when he got there; CCTV recorded his arrival and departure from the safe house in Kent; from there he had been tracked to the garage by an eye in the sky and even when he had stopped for petrol, he was filmed filling up the car.

CCTV is Big Brother's equivalent of a Kalashnikov rifle and, as if all this electronic surveillance was not enough, in between, he had found himself trapped in a car with Cassandra von Deker. More than once he had caught her looking at him as if he were some sort of specimen there to be analysed and dissected. And more than once he had seen her give him that strange look that he had encountered in the eyes of other women.

Jacks was of the opinion that George Orwell should never have written *1984* in doing so he told the powers-that-be how *not* to create Big Brother. In being so informed, the powers-that-be created a much gentler, caring version, one readily accepted by the majority on the grounds that the security is designed to make us feel safer. If you have nothing to hide then what have you to fear? was a popular conception but Jacks thought it an odd man or woman who did not have something they thought best kept hidden.

If only the fact that they picked their noses.

In the end, Orwell's pathetic hero Winston Smith learned to love Big Brother, but Jacks was determined no such thing would ever happen to him. He would hate Big Brother until the moment that certain bullet caught up with him and love and hate no longer mattered.

Full of thought, Jacks undressed for his third shower of the day and when he went into the bathroom, he had to smile at how well Jacob took care of those in need of refuge from the storm. When it came to refurbishing the Ladbroke Grove premises, Jacob had spared no expense. The large deep bath was straight out of the Savoy Hotel and when Jacks turned on the shower, he was sprayed hot water from three sides. The shower came equipped with an array of shampoos and he chose the first one to hand, revelling in the pleasure as he lathered his hair then his whole body. His senses were fully active and it seemed like he could feel every lance of water that caused his flesh to tingle, smell every nuance in the perfumed shampoo while the spray roared in his ears.

When Jacks came out of the shower, drying himself with a large white towel from a hot rail, he was in a settled state of mind. He knew al-Hashashin were out to kill Cassandra and he now knew for a certainty that they would now be out to kill him. He had identified the enemy for himself and knowing exactly who he was up against gave him much satisfaction.

Better the enemy you know than the enemy you don't. Such knowledge is no guarantee of victory, but if you were to die at least you would know who was killing you.

As Cassandra showered, her thoughts eventually settled on the man in the next room, the one she had come to think of as being a savage sophisticate. He was certainly not like any other man she had ever met. Nor like any other bodyguard. Other bodyguards worked to her instructions: this one had been running her since first she met him. Not only had she allowed him to do so, but she was enjoying being in his hands. Considering the ultra dangerous position she was in, it was strange that she now felt safer than she ever had in her life, a life she already owed to her protector. He could claim that he had killed three men so that he could live on, but in saving his own life, he had also saved hers. Her guardian could be ruthless, but he could also be gentle and caring. Considering that he had just killed three men, how considerate he was of her when she had her little accident. How considerate and how cold blooded. Had she not known that he had just killed three men she would never have guessed in a thousand years. His hands had been steady, his voice calm and modulated; his eyes perhaps more distant but they harboured no regret. As fearfully excited as *she* had been, she wondered if perhaps his heart had been beating louder in his chest. He claimed not to have a heart, but he was not fooling her, everybody had a heart. His was shielded by a wall of indifference, but there was not a wall built that could not be demolished and she wanted more than her life from this man, she wanted to find a way to his heart. Without first finding the way to his heart, no matter how wide open she left the gates, no matter how she flowered the pathways, he would never find the way to hers.

And it suddenly meant so much to her that he did.

Cassandra got out of the shower full of resolution, but within moments her uncertainty had crept back up on her. She did not need her disguise while in this house, so did she paint her face as usual, or did she stay as she was, with a minimum of make-up? And, after that, did she dress in the best she had brought along, did she stay casual, did she try for the sexy or the demure? The more she puzzled, the more certain she became that he would notice whatever way she came at him and in that knowledge she decided to come at him as the character he had created.

For now, she would be the girl; when the time came, she would be the woman.

* * *

Seated at a desk in his room in the al-Qaeda safe house in Paris, Azrael slowly closed the laptop computer he had been studying for the previous fifteen minutes, a time when he learned that the fools in London had again failed to kill the target and, even more disappointing, failed to kill the hated Mister Jacks. It seemed that Jacks killed the trio sent to kill him. Azrael knew the three men and he was not surprised that Bakri should fall, he never truly had what it took, but the other two were good which meant that Jacks had to be at least twice as good.

Azrael began by being angry that Jacks had survived, but he ended by being somewhat

77

pleased. It would have been good to hear that Jacks no longer walked the earth but the way things now stood, it would be he, Azrael, who would take his legs from under him. He had been ordered on to Luxemburg where he would kill Jacks as he had come to believe he was destined to do. And when he did kill the man who had killed his mentor, he hoped to make a film long to be remembered.

A target like Mister Jacks deserved at least a minor masterpiece.

★ ★ ★

In an upstairs room of the CIA's London offices, Special Agent Grant contacted control in Langley, Virginia. When the connection was made and Majors' image appeared on the computer monitor, after the obligatory greetings, Grant said, 'Our boy is doing really well. I'd like to know how he took out the three in the garage. Three went in, none came out; we have to tick them off as dead. I make that five he's taken out, the Hashashin brigade won't be too pleased with him.'

'Nothing from the Fox?' Majors asked.

'No,' Grant responded. 'And I'm not expecting much if anything. Mister Jacks isn't one of Jacob's regular people. They're friends from a way back. He'll be playing this one close to his chest.'

'Doesn't he always?' Majors asked. 'Where's our boy now?'

'No doubt tucked up in a safe house,' Grant replied. 'Probably Harry's.'

'And tomorrow?' Majors questioned.

'Our boy's running short of time.' Grant responded. 'I reckon tomorrow he goes for getting out of the country. Plane, boat or train and my money's on the latter. They can either travel separately on Euro Tunnel from London all the way to Brussels then rent a car when they get there, or they travel together with the car from Folkestone through the Channel Tunnel to Calais.'

'What do you think?' Majors asked.

'If it was me,' Grant replied. 'I'd stay together and with the car.'

Majors was silent for a moment and then he asked, 'Do you think our boy can make it all the way to Luxemburg?'

'My money's on him,' Grant replied. 'We can't follow him physically. If he spotted us, he would just as likely shoot us as tell us the time. We can't cover him along the way, but we can offer him discreet back up when he gets to the bank. Should he fail and the Deker woman is killed then Plan 'B' is ready to be activated at a moment's notice.'

'We need to get this one right,' Majors warned. 'Deker Industries cannot be allowed to fall into the hands of al-Qaeda.'

'It won't,' Grant concluded with assurance.

8

Jacks chose to dine wearing a luxurious, white towelling robe over a pair of black trousers and black socks. When Cassandra responded to his knock, she was wearing a simple pearl-grey dress that set off the locket at her slender neck, bare-legged in a pair of low-heeled black shoes, and her hair was tied up exposing the perfect symmetry of her oval, somewhat pale face. As simple as her dressing looked she had spent care and time to look as she did, but the hope of any compliment she might receive was dashed when Jacks asked her if she was ready before informing her that he was so hungry his stomach thought his throat had been cut.

Yet again, Cassandra found herself following Jacks. This time, he led her downstairs then through a door that led into a discreetly lit dining-room. All the chairs were up on bare tables except for the two chairs at a far corner candle-lit table laid out for dinner for two.

Cassandra smiled at the delight of it all; Jacks smiled because he knew Harry was getting him at it. At heart, Harry was a romantic who was forever trying to inflict his condition on others.

Jacks saw Cassandra seated and she watched, puzzled, as he collected another chair and set it at their table. 'Are we expecting someone else?' she asked.

'He's already here,' Jacks replied, as he produced his gun from a deep pocket of the dressing-gown. 'Meet Ivor Johnson,' he invited, as he laid the pistol on the chair then sat down, checking that it was in easy reach.

'Do you always take your friend out to dinner?' Cassandra asked, with a hint of a smile.

'Smile if you like,' Jacks said invitingly. 'But the fact is that although I believe I'm sitting in the safest safe house in the world, I could be wrong. For all we know, your maid planted two tracking devices on you and right now an army is surrounding this house. If they suddenly burst into the dining-room, then I don't want to be sitting here with just a steak knife in my hand. Be prepared. One I learned from the Boy Scouts.'

'You were a Boy Scout?' Cassandra asked, with evident disbelief.

Jacks shook his head. 'No, I was never a member, but that didn't forbid me from learning from them. Fact is, I have never read their motto as a bit of friendly advice on how to get through life. I've always read Be Prepared as a threat wrapped round a warning. And it's a warning I heed to this day . . . '

Jacks tailed off as Harry appeared through a swing door, bearing a large mug of coffee that he laid before Jacks. 'Would the young lady want something to drink? A glass of wine perhaps.'

For a reason she could not grasp, Cassandra looked towards Jacks and only when he consented with a nod did she ask for a small glass of red wine, stopping herself just in time from asking for a rare vintage, requesting instead whatever Harry thought was good enough, just so long as it wasn't too dry.

'I know just the one,' Harry responded with a certain pleasure. 'And to eat. What would you like?'

'I'm not really hungry,' Cassandra replied automatically before she realized how empty her stomach was. 'But I could try something,' she amended. 'What do you recommend?'

'Fish or meat?' Harry asked, and eventually Cassandra settled for Welsh lamb chops, new potatoes and whatever greens were available.

As Harry departed for the swing door, Cassandra said, 'I notice that Harry brought you a coffee. Are you like a policeman in that you never drink on the job?'

Cassandra asked the question lightly and she was taken aback when Jacks threw her a look carrying a hint of anger. 'I'm nothing like a policeman,' he stated coldly. 'And my job has nothing to do with my not drinking. I just don't drink. Period. Alcohol confuses the senses,' he continued. 'And, if you listen to my old friend Jacob, it's bad for the soul.'

Cassandra was on the verge of telling Jacks what a strange man he was but she was saved from making such a mistake by Harry reappearing, wielding a silver tray bearing a bottle of wine, a corkscrew and a highly polished glass. When he reached the table, Jacks and Cassandra, each somewhat amused, watched intently as he went through the ceremony of opening the bottle and pouring some into Cassandra's glass for her to taste and to savour.

Cassandra had practised the ceremony a thousand times and she sniffed the bouquet in which she detected a hint of clear blue skies and when she tasted it, the taste brought life to her palate. She was too well brought up to spit out the mouthful she tasted, instead she swallowed it with relish then held out her glass for more. 'Delicious,' she declared, as Harry filled her glass, giving Jacks a sidelong glance before departing once more for the swing door.

'You've made Harry's night,' Jacks observed. 'I could only wonder if you were as gracious with the servants back home.'

Cassandra delayed answering by first taking a sip of wine. 'Perhaps not,' she confessed eventually. 'But you don't know what servants can be like.'

'And that's a fact,' Jacks owned. 'Listen . . . ' he went on, his voice lowering as he drew closer to Cassandra, 'I have a lot to tell you, but before Harry gets here with Ye Food, I'm curious about something. Can I ask you a question?'

Hope gently blossomed inside Cassandra as she imagined he was going to ask of her something intimate. 'Ask me anything you like. I'll tell you anything you want to know,' she responded, in the tone of one ready to bare her heart.

'Right,' Jacks said. 'Tell me this: are you aware of the great ironies that have you hemmed in?'

Expecting Jacks to ask her something personal if not intimate, Cassandra was thrown sideways. 'The ironies?' she questioned, in obvious confusion. 'Whatever are you talking about?'

'That means you're missing it all,' Jacks said, giving Cassandra a regretful look. 'Irony is Fate's way of telling you that she takes an

85

interest in your life. And the way she's wrapped you up, she must be taking a great interest.'

'I still don't know what you're talking about,' Cassandra complained.

'I'm talking about three Heckler and Kochs and Mr Ivor Johnston over there. Remember the guns at the garage? The three on the table?'

Cassandra nodded, 'I saw them.'

'Heckler and Koch USP9s fitted with Brügger and Thornet sound suppressors. Best in the world. Over the counter fifteen hundred US. Under the counter anything up to five thousand,' Jacks began, all the while looking Cassandra in the eyes. 'These are specialist weapons, used by the major task-forces in the world. The USP9 was designed to kill a man in almost absolute silence. The guns and silencers at the garage were carrying matching serial numbers which means they came in a package. There is only one arms dealer in Europe who supplies them — Deker Industries — and considering that you've been living off the company all your life, that you will soon own it, it could be said that you sold three guns to three men so they could kill you with them. The money you got for them probably bought you a designer dress. I can only wonder what the killers have been doing with the guns.'

Jacks's words exploded in Cassandra's head like hand grenades as physically she retreated from his onslaught, sitting as far back in her chair as she could.

'And the irony doesn't end there,' Jacks went on. 'Mister Ivor Johnson there is also a specialist weapon. It's a marksman's pistol, a kind some use at Bisley. Like the Heckler and Kochs it's not an easy weapon to come by but one route is by way of Deker Industries. So, you not only sold three guns to your would-be killers, you also sold a gun to me so I could use it to kill those trying to kill you. Is there not certain perfection in the irony? Now that you're aware of it, it should be cutting you to ribbons.'

'It is,' Cassandra said, eyes down. 'I have to confess that I completely missed the irony of my situation. I appreciate your point but did you have to be so hurtful when you made it?'

'It wasn't me who was being hurtful,' Jacks parried, 'it was the truth.'

'OK,' Cassandra conceded. 'Then did you need to wield the truth like a hammer?'

'Truth carries its own weight,' Jacks countered. 'If it fell heavy that's because it was.'

'You're very clever with words, aren't you?' Cassandra said, as though accusing Jacks of a crime. 'Always got an answer.'

'Perhaps for you, I could develop a stutter,' Jacks came back, knowingly paraphrasing a line from a Bogart movie. And as he said it, he smiled; nothing delighted him more than to lift a good line from a movie and then incorporate it into real life . . . whatever that was.

Cassandra did not recognize the line, but she smiled wide in the light of Jacks's smile as, for a moment, his face lost its menace, his brow lost its furrows and his steel eyes softened. For that moment, it was like seeing the boy who still lived inside him and in seeing Jacks so revealed, Cassandra's heart went out to him, carrying with it a certain longing, a certain desire.

The moment passed and for Cassandra it was like seeing a grey veil drop over his face. 'You should smile more often,' she suggested.

'I'll bear that in mind,' Jacks responded with a smile that didn't quite reach his eyes.

Harry arrived bearing dinner, Cassandra's lamb complete with mint sauce, came on a china plate, Jacks's steak came on a salver complete with buttered mash and wild mushrooms. 'Enjoy,' Harry said, as he returned from whence he came. 'Anything else, just call out.'

Jacks attacked the steak with a vengeance

and while she ate her chops in the lady-like fashion she had been raised to do, watching Jacks eat so voraciously made her think that her description of him being the savage sophisticate was very apt, the savage first, and then the sophisticate.

Jacks swallowed a mouthful of steak and mushrooms and said, 'When I was showering I reviewed your situation and I reckon it's time you learned exactly what's going on. Who do you think wants to see you dead?'

'Someone on the board at Deker Industries,' Cassandra answered, as she savoured the taste of tender Welsh lamb.

'Why?' Jacks questioned, as he relished the taste of fried wild mushrooms. 'What's in it for him?'

'Money and power?'

'A full al-Hashashin assassination squad tried to take you out,' Jacks said informingly. 'They can be hired for private work, but you'd need at least a half-million sterling to even get their attention, so your suspect on the board doesn't need money and in his position, he probably has power enough. So forget a personal attack. If it was just one man out to see you dead, this would be an easy run, but I'm afraid it's much more serious. The three in Kensington, the three in the garage were al-Hashashin hitmen and they were sent by al-Qaeda.'

'My God,' Cassandra breathed, putting a hand to her throat. 'Al-Qaeda?'

'The same,' Jacks confirmed. 'It looks like they have a man on the board. You die, the board inherits and gradually all the top positions are in the hands of al-Qaeda's people. Do you know what it would mean if al-Qaeda controlled Deker Industries? It would mean that never again would they have to deal on the black-market. It would mean that they could have an order legally delivered to any port in the world. And I'm not just talking about Heckler, Koch, Ivor Johnson and Mister Kalashnikov. Deker Industries supplies *everything* military, from an armoured car all the way up to jet planes, bullets, bombs, missiles. With such an armoury behind them, al-Qaeda would be as well equipped as any modern army and, by way of them, so would Hezbollah, Hamas, the Taliban and all the others. With such weaponry, *jihad* would truly begin.'

'You paint a frightening picture,' Cassandra said, before draining her third glass of wine. 'What are we going to do?'

'What indeed?' Jacks questioned with an ironic smile. 'We can't fight al-Qaeda and win. The entire might of the US of A has been trying to do as much for a long time now and they haven't even come close. The people trying to kill us are al-Hashashin and we can't beat them either. In their world it's easier to find an assassin than a plumber. We're outnumbered all over; we could never win the war, but we could win this battle. When I get you safe to your bank, I strongly suggest that once you have proved who you are that you write a will immediately that in the event of your death, sudden or otherwise, would put Deker Industries beyond the reach of al-Qaeda. Do that, let it be known and you'll be safe enough.'

'But you won't be, will you?' Cassandra asked somewhat sagely. 'My death would no longer profit them, but they would still want to kill you even if only in revenge for killing their men.'

'I was born unsafe,' Jacks replied, pushing away the now empty salver. 'It's my natural, on-going condition. For a while now there has always been someone, somewhere who would like to see me dead . . . I should worry about al-Hashashin? What's a couple of hundred assassins here or there?' he concluded, smiling in the face of his own dark humour.

'God,' Cassandra said in a slightly slurred voice, 'you're so brave.'

Jacks shook his head. 'No I'm not, I'm

fearless and that's something else altogether. A brave man first has to conquer fear; I have no fear to conquer. It's part of my condition. Throw in the fact of my death wish and you end up with a man who is anything but brave. Don't be making a hero out of me because I'm anything but.'

'Whatever you say,' Cassandra countered, made bolder by the wine, 'you saved my life today. Without your protection I would be dead. If I want to make a hero out of you, then that's my right.'

Jacks smiled a most sincere smile. 'Make of me what you like,' he invited. 'I've been called worse things than a hero ... but just remember that I'm not really one. Come the end, I don't really care one way or the other.'

But Jacks was not fooling Cassandra for a moment. 'If you say so,' she said drily and then broached a subject that had crossed her mind more than once. 'Can I ask *you* something?'

'I'm holding my breath,' Jacks smiled in reply.

'I've noticed how fond you are of attacking capitalism,' she began accusingly, 'but you don't seem to mind capitalizing on your undoubted talents. So tell me, how much are you being paid to protect me?'

'You don't think I'm doing this for money,

do you?' Jacks replied, giving Cassandra a cold look. 'You couldn't pay me enough to do this job. I'm protecting you as a favour for a friend; when I need money I just look under the mattress.'

Cassandra looked at Jacks in a kind of awe. 'You're protecting me as a favour for a friend . . . ' she repeated softly, ingesting every word. 'You're a remarkable man.'

'If you say so,' Jacks retorted, putting a hand on top of Cassandra's wine glass as she lifted the bottle. 'And that's enough of that,' he instructed. 'We have a busy day ahead tomorrow,' he went on, looking directly into Cassandra's liquid green eyes. 'Who knows, it may even prove as exciting as today has been. But, for now, I want to have a word with Harry. You go on upstairs. I'll wake you tomorrow when the time is right. Try and get as much sleep as you can. Make the best of the soft bed. Who can say what tomorrow night will bring?'

Cassandra smiled a small smile. 'It's been a long time since I was sent upstairs and told to go to bed,' she said in a soft voice.

Jacks smiled in return. 'I'd come up and tuck you in but I'm not very good at that sort of thing. But I will say night, night, Cassandra.'

'Night, night to you, whoever you are,'

Cassandra came back, as she rose to her feet a little unsteadily; then, aware of Jacks's eyes on her every step of the way, left the dining-room with as much dignity as she could muster.

9

Jacks did not truly want to see Harry; saying he did was merely a ploy that enabled him to avoid having to say goodnight to Cassandra outside her bedroom door. Underneath the polished veneer she was a fragile girl and with half a bottle of wine as an incentive, she was likely to get emotional, and the last thing he needed right now was an offer from a woman he could only refuse, or to see the tears of a big girl.

Jacks gave it five minutes, collected his Ivor Johnson and went upstairs, a man full of thought and realization. With al-Qaeda being behind a plot to take control of the largest arms company in the world, it was as good as certain that someone beyond Jacob and himself knew what was going on. Jacob would no doubt be keeping MI5 and MOSSAD up to date but Jacks suspected that the CIA was in there somewhere and that they would need no one to keep *them* up to date.

If he knew the CIA as well as he thought he did, then they probably kicked off ahead of the field and, with so many other agencies likely to be interested in the plot, Jacks was starting to feel like a man in a queue who has no idea of how many are in front of him nor of how many are behind.

Like all the rooms in the safe house, Jacks's came complete with a PC and, foregoing speculation for the moment, he made a cup of coffee, sat down and clicked on to the Internet. Aeroplanes and boats were out and he clicked on to the website for the Channel Tunnel which offered him a choice of two runs: Eurostar that ran all the way from London to Brussels in two hours fifteen minutes or Eurotunnel that ran from Folkestone to Calais in thirty-five minutes.

After but a moment's thought, Jacks chose Folkestone. Not only was the tunnel the quickest, with fifty-three loading times a day, it meant that they could choose their time while staying with the car. Customs was all done the English side of the water which meant that even if they were expected at the Calais end, with the car they at least would have a chance to make a run of it.

Decision made, Jacks then switched on to a website for Luxemburg. It was not a country he knew much about and the first thing he learned was that it was *not* a country. Luxemburg was a Province of Belgium and considering Belgium's European reputation, Jacks was not too sure what that said about the place. Next thing Jacks discovered was that Luxemburg was a land-locked island enclosed by the borders of France, Belgium and Germany which meant there were many ways in and out of the place: it would just be a matter of picking the right one.

Research done, decisions made, Jacks switched off the computer and rang Jacob on the cloned mobile. 'Did you learn anything from the laptop?'

'My people are working on it,' Jacob replied. 'According to them, someone tried to crash it, but they're confident that they can crack the codes and passwords then trace it back to source. And the BMW would seem to be the property of an off-shore investment company registered in the Cayman Islands.'

'The Heckler and Kochs?'

'Part of a consignment that went missing on their way to a Special Forces group in Afghanistan,' Jacob answered. 'Not a lot of help, I'm afraid.'

'I was curious about the guns,' Jacks said. 'Tell me, do you know if they came by way of Deker Industries?'

'Of course,' Jacob sighed in reply. 'Messrs Heckler and Koch only travel with the best. A certain irony there, I'm sure you agree.'

'I already pointed it out to the package,' Jacks responded. 'She was quite upset to learn that she had essentially sold her killers the guns with which to kill her.'

'I'm sure you spelled it all out for her,' Jacob said drily. 'How's she bearing up?'

'Not too bad,' Jacks said thoughtfully. 'She's not long eaten a hearty meal, drunk some wine; by now she should be sound asleep. Tomorrow we move, and I could use some help on that front.'

'Just ask,' Jacob stated.

'Starting from nine in the morning book tickets for Mister Jacks and Cassandra von Deker to fly out of every major airport in Britain. Vary the times and destinations in Europe. I don't reckon to fool the enemy, but I can spread them thin on the ground. They'll know that all the bookings can't be real and doubt if even one is but they'll need to check just in case I'm not bluffing.'

'Consider it done.'

'Then do the same with Eurostar and Eurotunnel. Spread the bookings over the day and while there, make a real booking for around three o'clock on Eurotunnel,' he concluded, giving Jacob the names on two forged passports. 'It's only a thirty-five minute crossing and it's a free run the other side. Now tell me this, I presume that the British know enough of what's going on, that MOSSAD knows everything that's going on and that the CIA think they do, so I'm assuming that if I get it wrong there's a contingency plan waiting to fall into place.'

'There's always a contingency plan,' Jacob declared. 'It's a rule of the game.'

'Of course it is,' Jacks agreed. 'And what's the word on the maid?'

'She's dead,' Jacob replied. 'You turning up at the safe house must have alarmed her. She had a mobile camera phone hidden in a suitcase, but she had already removed the chip and destroyed it. When she was being questioned she asked to go to the bathroom and while in there, behind a locked door, she swallowed what Carter suspects as being a cyanide capsule . . . Carter sends his apologies for doubting your suspicions about her.'

'Hell,' Jacks sighed. 'She was only a girl; I really don't understand religious fanaticism. But then, there's a lot of human behaviour that I don't understand.'

'Who can say with people?' Jacob asked in reply. 'It may interest you to know that the three from the garage were all on someone's list. MOSSAD were particularly pleased to hear of the demise of one.'

'I already knew they were the bad guys, Jacob,' Jacks said shortly. 'I don't care if they were number one on the FBI's Most Wanted, there's no need to justify my actions. I justified them well in advance,' he went on, a hint of anger in his tone. 'The means justify the end and the end desired here is that I stay alive, because if I fall then the package doesn't get unwrapped gently, Messrs Heckler and Koch will rip her open. I'm not doing this for the medals; I'm doing this as a favour for you.'

'I know,' Jacob sighed. 'Forgive me if I appeared to be trying to help you justify your actions. You have no need of justification. You will survive this,' he predicted. 'We all want to live: you *need* to live. It's your need to live so that someone else might live that is your driving force. It's your way of justifying your existence.'

'Well,' Jacks drawled, 'I never knew that and here was me thinking I was just a killer who only killed people who were intent on killing him. I learn something new every day!'

Jacob chuckled over the phone. 'You're an interesting man, no doubt about that,' he judged. 'Is there anything else I can do for you?'

'Not for now,' Jacks replied. 'I'll contact you tomorrow when we're in France.'

'I'll be anticipating hearing from you,' Jacob stated. 'Be Prepared!'

'You're talking to the original Boy Scout,' Jacks retorted, then terminated the call.

Across the hallway, curled up in bed in the foetal position, Cassandra von Deker was anything but sound asleep, the excitements of the day, the fears and the memories had caught up with her and for the last hour or so she had been as restless as a leopard caught in a trap. She felt so lonely; tonight was probably the first night in her life where there was not at least a maid within calling distance. There was a man across the hallway who had sworn to guard her life, but he was not the man to go to in loneliness. From what she had seen and heard, loneliness was his natural condition; he would not understand what her problem was because it revolved around a need he did not appear to have. She had never met a man like him before. Her experience of men was limited but she was certain that even if she had known a thousand she would never before have met a man like the one they called Mister Jacks. All the men she had met began by being afraid of her power position, or being over impressed by her wealth, but beside the man across the way, she was powerless and her wealth did not impress him one bit; if anything, it offended him.

As her restlessness grew, as on many other nights, under the bedcover her right hand found its way between her thighs. On other occasions, her fantasies had revolved round the dominant female and the submissive male, but tonight the roles were subtly reversing themselves until it was she who lay at the mercy of the man across the hallway, the one with the deep brown eyes that saw right through her, the one with the slender hands of a pianist, and it was the thought of those killer hands, touching her where she was touching herself that finally threw her over the top, bringing her to bite into the pillow lest she cry aloud as her body shuddered then re-shuddered in wonderful release.

It was normal for Cassandra to cry as she came, but usually she shed a few solitary tears that seemed to take forever to run down her cheeks but tonight her tears flowed freely, rushing down her cheeks until she found herself sobbing into a tightly held pillow.

The aftermath of ecstasy brought her the stillness she needed and very shortly she drifted off into a deep sleep that lay rooted in physical and emotional exhaustion.

Her final thoughts evolved from the fact that she had lived more during the previous twelve hours or so than she seemed to have lived in her life.

Which was odd, considering that all day she had been walking hand in hand with Death.

10

Jacks had set his mental alarm clock for 7.00 a.m. and when it went off, he instantly awoke. He had read and heard of people who could wake and then turn over and go back to sleep and he had often wondered how they stilled their minds in order to do so, assuming in the first place that their minds woke up.

His stainless-steel Omega watch read 7.05 a.m. and, as he got out of bed and realized that his alarm clock was running five minutes late, he smiled to think he must be slipping. From there, he showered, shampooed, shaved, dressed, made a black coffee which he sipped as he sat before the PC, clicking on to the net in search of a map of Kent. The most direct route to Folkestone was by way of the M20 but motorways have a camera planted on almost every bridge so he chose a more indirect country route. They were not due in Folkestone until 2.30 p.m. which gave him plenty of time to get there and time enough to prepare the package for what was certain to lay ahead. Either before Luxemburg, at Luxemburg or both, al-Hashashin were honour bound to go for a hit; it was a time for being prepared.

The route to Folkestone imprinted on his mind, he switched off the computer then used an internal phone to ring downstairs to Harry.

'Good morning,' Harry said. 'Will it be breakfast for two?'

'Nine o'clock,' Jacks defined. 'Ring the girl and tell her I'll give her a knock.'

'The usual?' Harry questioned.

'The usual,' Jacks responded. 'Ask the girl what she wants when you ring her.'

'See you at nine,' Harry concluded, but Jacks had terminated the call before he said it.

Jacks asked Harry to ring Cassandra simply because he himself could not ring her. There were no room to room phone connections: only Harry could ring a room direct. Unfortunately, Cassandra did not know this and on receiving Harry's call she foolishly thought that for some reason, her guardian was not speaking to her.

Cassandra was awake when she got the call. After her restless beginning the night before, she had drifted off into a deep sleep from which she awoke feeling fully refreshed. A shower and a coffee did their bit and she had to own that she was feeling quite vital. For some reason, she thought that with death lurking round the corner she should not be feeling so alive and then she realized that her vitality was a product of her situation. The knowledge that she could be dead before the day was out was a great reason for being alive.

And to think that her protector spent most of his life living out times like these. By now he must be addicted to danger, and if this was the case then that did not leave much space for her; the last thing she would ever want was to be a danger to him.

She was anything but dangerous; fortunately the man across the hallway was dangerous enough for both of them.

When Jacks knocked on Cassandra's door, she opened it with a friendly smile that was barely returned. 'You set?' Jacks asked.

'I hope so,' Cassandra replied, as she closed the door and fell into step beside him, daring to take him by an arm as they made their way downstairs. He flinched at her intrusion and slipped free first step into the dining-room. 'It's just that you make me feel safe,' she explained, as she sat at the table laid for breakfast.

'And that's why I'm here,' Jacks replied, as he sat down opposite, laying his Ivor Johnson on a spare chair. 'Now all I have to do is keep you that way.'

'I have great confidence in you,' Cassandra said truthfully.

'I hope for my sake that your confidence is justified,' Jacks came back.

Harry arrived bearing poached eggs on toast for Cassandra and a plate of something grey for Jacks that Cassandra did not recognize. 'What is that?' she enquired, as she watched him sprinkle sugar and pour milk over it.

'A long time ago,' Jacks replied, giving her an amused look, 'I knew a woman called Jacqueline who was only good at two things, I won't tell you what the first thing was but the second was making porridge. I passed the recipe on to Harry. Made with full cream milk, it's like having a pudding for breakfast,' he concluded, before savouring the first mouthful.

Seeing the childlike delight on Jacks's face, Cassandra asked him how many sides there were to his character and how did the boy inside him adjust to holding a gun in his hand.

'Easy,' Jacks replied. 'He just sees it all as a game of the Good Guys versus the Bad Guys. A game with no rules other than the ones he inflicts on himself. A very serious, deadly game where losing could cost him his life but a game for all that . . . You want to come out and play?'

The invite came out as a threat; the menace in Jacks's eyes sending a shiver up Cassandra's back. 'So long as I'm on your side and you're on mine,' she qualified. 'Any particular game in mind?'

'It's the same old one,' Jacks answered. 'Dodge the bullets but first dodge the cameras. Today we move into France by way of the tunnel. When we get to Folkestone the car will pop up on all kinds of security screens. The car's safe but I want you to keep your head down as much as you can. People will be trying to spot us.'

'Is it that easy to break into a security system?' Cassandra asked, as she tucked into her poached eggs.

'You have to know the right buttons to press,' Jacks answered, as he finished off his porridge. 'After that, it's simple. Did you know that CCTV is a world-wide network? Nobody needs physically to follow anyone anymore. You can watch a man board a plane on CCTV then watch him disembark at his destination, follow the cab all the way to his hotel and observe him as he checks in. Between satellite surveillance and CCTV it's almost impossible to dodge Big Brother. But we'll do our best.'

Cassandra smiled a small smile. 'But I have no papers.'

'Yes you have,' Jacks corrected. 'A passport and an international driving licence in another name. I'll give them to you before we leave along with two thousand euros and a thousand sterling. Should we get separated, you and your .45 will be able to move around.'

The thought of being separated from the man across the table alarmed Cassandra and she said, 'You'd never abandon me, would you?'

'Never by choice,' Jacks replied. 'It looks like you're stuck with me all the way to Luxemburg.'

'I can think of no other man I'd rather journey with,' Cassandra said sincerely.

'You're forgetting Brad Pitt,' Jacks said with a smile.

'He's an actor,' Cassandra said, smiling in turn, 'you're the real thing.'

'I'm certainly something,' Jacks conceded.

★   ★   ★

London born and bred, Jacks knew well the streets of the capital. When he and Cassandra left Ladbroke Grove behind he avoided having to drive through the West End with its armed policemen on patrol by heading east and then reaching South London by way of the Rotherhithe Tunnel. The tunnel brought him out into Bermondsey, the borough of his birth and, as he essentially drove by his first doorstep, he asked, 'Do you live in London or are you just visiting?'

'I have a flat in Belgravia,' Cassandra replied.

'Where else?' Jacks questioned drily.

'And I have an apartment in New York. Seventh Avenue,' she went on rubbing it in. 'And that's not to mention the family home in Berlin, or the estate by the Black Forest.'

Jacks chuckled in the face of Cassandra's obvious petulance. 'I'm so impressed,' he quipped, 'I'm almost taken aback.'

'You don't like the rich, do you?' Cassandra said accusingly.

'It's not the rich I don't like,' Jacks corrected. 'I like you. What I don't like is to what use you put your riches. Money is wasted on you simply because you have never known what it's like never to have had any. You'll spend twenty thousand on a frock where with that kind of money you could bring water to a thirsty African village. No imagination the rich; they think money is designed merely to make more money.'

'Being wealthy doesn't guarantee happiness,' Cassandra said defensively.

'Neither does being poor,' Jacks stated with a grin just for Cassandra. 'But the way I see it, if you have to be unhappy then better to cry in the back seat of a Rolls Royce than upstairs on a number seventeen bus and I bet you agree with that one!'

'Are you going to pick on me all the way to Luxemburg?' Cassandra wanted to know, as she gave Jacks a defiant look. 'Why are you always so hard on me?'

'Hard on you?' Jacks questioned in sincere surprise. 'You may think this is me being hard, but actually this is me at my most gentle. When I'm being hard on someone, I put a bullet in their head.'

Cassandra could find no answer to that. The man seated beside her had a way of stopping a conversation in its tracks much as he had a way of stopping people. He put a bullet in your head: it was a mental bullet but it still scrambled your brains.

But, much as he had told her off, in the midst of his mocking, he had told her that he liked her, and Cassandra found a comfort in this. If he felt enough to like her then perhaps he could come to feel much more.

Yet again, Jacks found himself driving down the Old Kent Road. This time he followed it all the way out of London into Kent where he got on the road for Bromley and from there to the town of Maidstone which he by-passed in favour of country lanes, all the while looking out for a quiet pub where they could get something to eat.

A couple of miles short of a place called Bearstead, Jacks smiled when he saw a sign advertising The Starving Rascal, a pub that offered home-cooked meals. 'Sounds like my kind of place,' he said with a grin. 'I don't know about being a rascal but I'm certainly starving. Porridge goes a long way but it doesn't go all day. What about you? Eat when you can is the first rule of survival.'

'I could eat something,' Cassandra owned. 'If my stomach will let me.'

'Butterflies?'

'Pterodactyls,' Cassandra corrected.

Jacks smiled as an image floated across his mind. 'You'll be all right,' he said, as instinctively he reached out his left hand and gave Cassandra's arm a reassuring squeeze. 'This time tomorrow, you'll have your life back.'

Jacks's grip spoke to Cassandra of strength and gentleness and she gave him a soft look as she said, 'It will be a different life,' she predicted. 'After you, life will never be the same.'

'There is that,' Jacks accepted as he turned into The Starving Rascal and parked round the back. Only one other car was in the car-park and Jacks automatically looked it over as he and Cassandra went into the pub.

A couple of locals checked them out over their pints before mine host led them through into a restaurant area that housed only two customers.

Jacks chose a table in a corner, sitting back to a wall from where he could observe the car-park and the way into the restaurant. He ordered a coffee, Cassandra did likewise and from the menu, he went for home-made cottage pie while Cassandra picked the poached Scottish salmon.

When they were served, Jacks said, 'Enjoy that because we don't know when, where or if we'll eat next. This is as safe as you'll be until we get there. Make the most of it.'

'How do you know we're safe?' Cassandra challenged, before savouring a mouthful of salmon. 'That couple over there,' she went on, nodding in their direction. 'How do you know they're not a threat?'

'Al-Hashashin is old-fashioned,' Jacks replied between forked mouthfuls of the most delicious pie. 'They don't enlist female assassins. Be grateful that they are so chauvinistic. They used your maid as an information source; they could just as easily have ordered her to kill you. Watch Hollywood movies and you'd come to believe that female assassins were falling out of the trees. I've been in the business a while and I know by reputation one or two top hitters around the world, but I've only ever heard of one woman. She works for the Russian Mafia, codenamed Catharine. They say she's ex-KGB but then they say a lot of things. Al-Qaeda, Hamas, Hezbollah and a few others are not averse to using female suicide bombers but in the world of al-Hashashin, killing is a man's job.'

'And in your world?' Cassandra questioned. 'Do women have a place there? One woman in particular perhaps?'

Jacks smiled all over his face. 'I was wondering when you'd get round to that one,' he claimed. 'Now, I could answer your question but, if I do, another question will follow then another and, before we know it, I'll be baring my soul. Not only am I reluctant to do such a thing but I don't have the time. Just eat up your lunch and then we'll get out of here.'

In response, Cassandra stared at Jacks for a long moment before saying, 'You're a hard man to reach.'

'Maybe it's a case of there being nothing there to reach,' Jacks suggested.

'Or too much,' Cassandra countered.

'You'll never know,' Jacks predicted.

★ ★ ★

From The Starving Rascal, Jacks drove straight for Folkestone. A couple of miles before reaching the port, he stopped at a service station and filled the car with petrol. When he went into the shop to pay the bill, he picked up a glossy magazine, a *Times* newspaper, a cheap Biro and seeing a rack of baseball-caps, he chose a black one bearing the initials NYC. As with many people, the al-Qaeda attack of 9/11 was deeply imprinted on Jacks's mind. A man he knew of in the CIA had been killed during the attack and where al-Qaeda had many reasons for targeting the Twin Towers, he had always thought that somewhere in their reasoning had been the knowledge that the old enemy, the CIA, occupied two floors of the South Tower.

Jacks returned to the car wearing the baseball cap. When Cassandra saw him wearing it she smiled and said, 'It isn't exactly you.'

'That's why I'm wearing it,' Jacks answered, as he handed her the glossy magazine. 'And this is for you.'

'*HELLO* magazine?' Cassandra questioned.

'You don't have to read it,' Jacks said as he laid *The Times* on his lap and pulled away from the service station. 'It's to hide behind. Folkestone Harbour has more cameras than

Hollywood. They'll be watching for us. So, when we get there, keep your head down.'

'I will,' Cassandra promised.

★ ★ ★

Back at al-Hashashin headquarters in London, Rimmon was becoming more concerned by the moment. It was getting late in the afternoon and there was still no sign of Jacks or the von Deker woman. Jacks had laid a false trail at almost every airport in England but Rimmon had decided to concentrate all his eyes on Folkestone Harbour one side and Calais, Coquelles International Terminal at the other. His computer people were hooked up to the CCTV system both sides but with no sign yet of the targets, he was beginning to think he had made the wrong choice. Either that or he had missed them coming through the tunnel and they were already well on their way across France. His people had inserted a profile of Cassandra von Deker into the CCTV system, but so far nothing like a match had registered on the screens.

'We've got her,' Achmir suddenly announced. 'They've just exited the French side.'

'Are you sure?' Rimmon wanted to know as he hurried for a look.

'Ninety-three per cent,' Achmir replied.

'The man driving is wearing a baseball cap pulled low; assuming it's Mister Jacks then we still don't know what he looks like. But the Deker woman looked directly into a camera. It's definitely her.'

Praise be to Allah, Rimmon thought, as he established what make of car Jacks was driving, the number plate then passed the information on to his men waiting in France.

Allah was kind.

★ ★ ★

Back at CIA headquarters in London, Special Agent Grant was in contact with his section chief back at Langley. 'I was right,' he stated. 'Our boy crossed by way of the tunnel. We almost missed him; if the woman doesn't look up at the wrong time, they make it clean.'

'But we didn't miss them,' Majors qualified. 'And if we didn't then it's unlikely that the other side did. I presume they'll be waiting.'

'They'll be waiting all right,' Grant agreed. 'But I reckon our boy will be expecting them. I have a couple of people in the area; if anything goes down, we'll hear about it fast.'

'Is your money still on Jacks?' Majors wanted to know.

'I wish I could increase my stake,' Grant said by way of reply. 'Jacks is the best I ever saw. He'll make it.'

'One can but hope,' Majors replied.

11

Fortunately, that afternoon everything was running smoothly at Folkestone Harbour. Jacks and Cassandra claimed their tickets, passed easily through passport control and after a short queue found themselves and the car ensconced in a railway carriage ready to journey underneath a sea. There were two CCTV cameras on the carriage and Jacks reminded Cassandra once more to keep her head down.

The rest of the carriage was occupied by half-a-dozen cars carrying Manchester United supporters on their way to some big match or other and where many would have felt unsafe in such company, Jacks felt safer than he had all day.

Beside Jacks, head down, for want of something better to do, Cassandra actually found herself reading the glossy celebrity magazine and the more she read the harder she found it to believe just how far people would go in betraying themselves and friends just so they could retain a fame that was itself hollow to begin with. She was not so young that she could not remember when the famous had actually done something to be famous for, but nowadays, judging by the magazine, you could become famous merely by changing the colour of the hair you were famous for.

As Cassandra shook her head in disbelief, when the high-speed train started moving, Jacks folded *The Times* newspaper the right way then, Biro in hand, set about doing the crossword. Solving *The Times* crossword was a daily ritual in Jacks's life. It was his way of keeping a check on the workings of his mind. Should he ever deteriorate to the point that he rarely solved a crossword in a week, he would know that he was losing it and then before he lost too much, decide what he was going to do in the face of his worsening condition.

The requisite time allowed for completion of the crossword was thirty minutes but thirty-five minutes later, when the train stopped at Calais, Coquelles International Terminal, he was still stuck on the final clue. What he needed was a thirteen-letter word that had some relation to the bowels but even though it was anagrammatic and he had only five spaces to fill, he could not place the remaining letters. Jacks liked to be beaten now and then, it showed that the compilers were doing their job, and he smiled as he thought that now he must definitely live until tomorrow. If he were to die today, he would die never knowing exactly what that thirteen-letter word was.

Cassandra kept her head down as they disembarked, she kept it down as they followed the queue out of the terminal, but, when Jacks put his foot down and they started moving faster, she raised her head from the magazine she'd been staring at and asked, 'Are we safe yet?'

'If we were,' Jacks replied, throwing her a sideward glance, 'we may not be now. We just passed two exit cameras and you were looking right at one.'

Cassandra flinched. 'I'm sorry,' she said in a small voice. 'I thought we were clear.'

'We almost were,' Jacks said, with a shake of his head. 'But really we have no way of knowing if anyone's even watching. We have to assume they are and if they are we have to assume that we've been spotted and that they're waiting on us to put in an appearance. Keep your eye on your mirror and I'll keep an eye on mine. And don't be sorry: they're just as likely to spot me as they are you.'

When they left the terminal, Jacks followed a road sign for Lille a town near the Belgian border. They drove out of the terminal into pouring rain being driven by a howling wind.

The windscreen wipers played a squeaky tune as Jacks put his foot down and the Focus betrayed the power it had hidden under the bonnet. Beside him, Cassandra caught her breath as he said, 'Didn't I tell you this was a Ferrari in disguise?'

'I believe you,' Cassandra said, as she held on tight.

The bad weather had brought an early darkness and Jacks welcomed it as a friend. If the darkness and the driving rain hindered his vision, then it hindered that of the enemy. If they had been spotted then the enemy knew that he was driving a dark blue Ford Focus, and they would probably know the number plate and when, thirty odd kilometres down the road, a black BMW pulled out of a lay-by and took up a position behind them, not too close to be an imminent threat but close enough to stay in touch, he figured that they had been spotted.

'The London Yardie gangs call a BMW Bad Man's Wheels,' Jacks observed. 'And I'm beginning to think they know something I don't,' he concluded as he put his foot down further on the accelerator, initially leaving the BMW behind but it soon caught up again. 'No doubt about it,' Jacks said, 'they're on to us. Reach under the dashboard, you'll find a switch there . . . '

'Got it,' Cassandra said.

'Flick it,' Jacks ordered.

As she did so, Cassandra asked, 'What does it do?'

'It stops the brake lights from coming on,' Jacks replied, as half a kilometre on, he braked suddenly and threw the Focus into a sharp right turn that led on to a slip road.

With no warning of Jacks's move to guide it, the black BMW sped on by and, as Jacks glanced back, he saw that it contained two men.

'That's clever,' Cassandra said.

'But not clever enough,' Jacks observed. 'The people in the BMW will be on the phone right now telling someone else our position. And they have no need to get behind us. Now that they know where we are all they have to do is wait up ahead. They'll know we'll have to stop somewhere either for fuel, food or for the night. If they're any good at what they do they'll have the roadside cafés and hotels staked out just waiting on us to show our faces.'

'What are we going to do?' Cassandra asked, with a hint of fear.

'Leave it to me, kid,' Jacks replied. 'I'm making this up as we go along, but I'm sure I'll think of something. I always do.'

Jacks had a great sense of direction and

though he weaved and turned for almost an hour, speeding through the countryside, he kept moving in a general easterly direction. Twice he drove back on to the main highway and off again; when he drove off the third time on seeing a sign for La Capelle he made a decision that led him to turn off the road and into a dimly lit service station.

'What are you doing?' Cassandra asked in alarm.

'I'm sick of running from these wimps,' Jacks enunciated, giving a cold smile as he borrowed a line from one of his favourite movies.

The lorry-park was quite full but the commercial area contained only four vehicles and when Jacks saw that one of the parked cars was a black BMW he grinned knowingly. 'I think our friends may be waiting for us inside,' he said, as he parked in a position that had him facing the right way in case he needed to get out of there fast.

Cassandra's heart leapt as it was kicked by a rush of fear. 'Then why don't we just drive on?' she asked, as Jacks switched off the engine.

'If we just keep driving,' he replied, 'in time, every car that's out hunting us will converge and we'll find ourselves boxed in with nowhere to go. It's time that we chased them. Time to break the pattern. Time to take the fight to them.'

'I'm frightened,' she said in a small voice.

'Trust me,' Jacks asked. 'Just follow my lead and do what I tell you to do,' he went on, as he checked his Ivor Johnson before putting it in a coat pocket and getting out of the car. Cassandra got out her side and Jacks offered her his left arm to hold on to as they fought their way through the rain that was still being driven by a howling wind.

Jacks knew that anyone watching for them would be seated where they had a view of the car-park and when he saw two shapes sitting by a window, he figured that he had located the enemy while at the same time knowing that they had seen him and Cassandra.

The café was almost empty. Jacks tied the eight boisterous youths sitting in a corner to the two Transit vans parked side by side, the elderly man to the Citroën which left the two men by the window belonging to the BMW.

Like all such places the service station café was festooned by mirrors and, as they approached the service counter, Jacks used one or two to keep an eye on the two men he believed were there to kill him.

In broken French, Jacks ordered two black coffees and, much to Cassandra's surprise, two double cheese-burgers to take away. The coffees came in foam containers, the burgers in a brown paper bag and when the bill was paid, Jacks told Cassandra to carry the tray with the coffees; he collected the burgers in his left hand then made her follow him to a pre-selected table.

The walk to the table was a long one and every step, holding the Ivor Johnson tightly in his pocket, Jacks was ready for the two men to make a move. They didn't and on reaching the selected table, he made Cassandra sit with her back to the two men while he sat where he could watch them in a mirror.

The two by the window were pros, they never even glanced his way and, under cover of the table, Jacks retrieved the Ivor Johnson from his pocket and slid it into the burger bag, pushing the barrel into the soft rolls before wrapping the brown paper round the handle and pushing his right forefinger through until he had a firm grip on the gun with his finger on the trigger.

'Drink your coffee,' he said to Cassandra, as he used his left hand to take a sip of his. As he did so, he saw that one of the men was using a mobile phone and he figured he was calling for back up. 'Drink it fast,' he continued, putting down his drink, leaning closer and laying his hand on hers, giving it a squeeze as he held her frightened eyes with a reassuring look. 'We're under threat,' he went on, smiling for anyone who might be watching, 'but I have things in check. When we stand up to leave, here's what I want you to do.'

Somewhat comforted by Jacks holding her hand, Cassandra listened to his instructions and when he asked her if she understood she said that she did but where she understood the instructions she had no idea as to why she had been given them.

Jacks figured that the two men by the window would wait until the back up arrived, hang on until Cassandra and he left the café then take them on the outside and, as he had no idea as to how close or how far away the back up was, he knew he had to move fast by offering the two by the window an opportunity they would be unable to pass up.

'Ready?' he asked as he stood, the Ivor Johnson gripped in his right hand.

Cassandra nodded fearfully, stood up, joined Jacks and the pair of them headed for the exit. Halfway there, as per instructions, Cassandra stopped by a sign indicating the toilets, making it obvious to anyone watching that she really needed to go. Jacks appeared to try to talk her out of it before surrendering with a reluctant shake of his head and following her through the door that led to the toilet area.

The Ladies was on the right of a corridor and, almost pushing Cassandra, he followed her in. The squeaky door opened to reveal two rows of cubicles separated by a double line of sinks. Jacks led Cassandra to a centre cubicle on the left. 'Stand on the seat and point the .45 at the door,' he whispered urgently. 'Same routine as the last time: anyone but me, shoot them. When you hear that door squeak, cough loudly,' and then without awaiting an answer he closed the door on her before taking up a position at the end of the sink divide, standing there his back pressed to cold tiles, waiting as he so often had waited before. As fortune would have it, there was a chrome condom machine on the wall facing him that gave him a somewhat distorted view of the entrance door and he tensed himself in preparation for what he believed was inevitable.

Standing there on a toilet seat .45 grasped in both hands, Cassandra was more afraid than she had ever thought it possible for her to be. In her chest, her heart was beating so loud she thought the world must be hearing it and her mouth was as dry as the Gobi.

When the entrance door squeaked, her cough came out as a croak.

12

The first assassin into the Ladies hunkered down on the side the cough had come from and started to look under the cubicle doors, the second stood with his back to the squeaky door, a gun held ready in his right hand.

Watching the distorted reflection in the chrome condom dispenser, Jacks waited until the one on the floor reached the middle of the row of cubicles then, holding his breath, in one fluid movement he stepped out, raised the burger bag and shot the one at the door between the eyes. The one on the floor had made the mistake of taking his weight on the heel of the hand holding his gun and, as he struggled to raise it, looking up directly into Jacks's face, Jacks shot him through his left eye. The move took no more than two seconds and both men were dead before they hit the floor. The improvised silencer of cheeseburgers and brown paper bag deadened the noise the Ivor Johnson made but the audible popping sound it emitted echoed and re-echoed off the bare toilet walls.

Inside the chosen cubicle, Cassandra stood on the toilet seat trembling from head to toe.

At the sound of the shots, coming so close together as to be almost simultaneous, she almost fainted from the great intake of fear that swamped her whole system. When Jacks whispered her name and pushed open the cubicle door she as good as fell into his arms.

'It's all right,' Jacks said, supporting her with his left arm. 'But we've got to get out of here,' he went on, retrieving the .45 from her ice-cold fingers and returning it to her canvas bag. 'Hold on just a bit longer,' he coaxed, as he took her by the left hand and led her out of the Ladies.

This time around, Cassandra saw the bodies and the blood. She had to step over a man who was minus the back of his head and she caught her breath when Jacks pulled the one by the exit door out of the way to reveal a streak of blood mixed with torn flesh and mangled brains.

The corridor outside was empty and instead of turning back into the café area, with Cassandra holding tightly to his left hand, Jacks turned towards a fire exit situated at the far end. A push on the security bar and he pulled Cassandra out into the still driving rain, the still howling wind.

The fire exit led out into the lorry-park and, hugging a wall, Cassandra still holding tight to his left hand, Ivor Johnson gripped in his right, Jacks made his way to the car-park. He was just about to step out from the security of the wall when he saw another black BMW pull in, stepping back as he watched it park beside the first one there.

As the two men in the car got out, joining each other at the front of the car Jacks noted that both had their right hands buried in coat pockets. He watched them walk, heads down towards the café entrance and when he saw they were going to use the parked Transit vans as cover from the wind-driven rain, he let go of Cassandra's hand, whispered, 'Wait here,' then ran towards the two men. He was wearing soft-soled shoes and what with the cover of the screeching wind and a diesel lorry revving up behind him, the two men never heard him coming. Timing his move when the men were halfway between the Transits, he came to a halt, raised the Ivor Johnson in its improvised silencer and called, 'Cherchez vous pour moi?'

The one on Jacks's left reacted first, drawing a gun from his coat pocket before coming round the long way: Jacks shot him through the left temple. The second man, hampered by his partner to his left and the Transit van to his right, was slower, but he died just as quickly when Jacks's second bullet hit him in the back of his head then destroyed his face on the way out.

The wind still howled, the diesel engine still revved and Jacks stood a moment listening for an outcry. When none came, he dropped the burger bag, kicked it under the right Transit van then, Ivor Johnson tucked away inside his coat, ran back to Cassandra to find her ashen-faced, back pressed tightly against the brick wall. 'Come on,' he said urgently as he took her by a hand.

'I can't move,' Cassandra responded in a voice layered with panic. 'My legs won't obey me.'

'Of course you can move,' Jacks stated, as he came in close and Cassandra found herself staring into his black, burning eyes, gasping as he pulled her away from the wall before dragging her across the car-park to the parked Focus, clicking the locks open before opening the passenger door and bundling her uncaringly into the car.

As Jacks got into the Focus, he had a quick look around but seeing no sign of discovery, he switched on and pulled out of the service station at the speed of a man in no hurry to get anywhere. Once free of the service station, out on the open road, he put his foot down and sped off in the direction of the Luxemburg border.

'Put your seat belt on,' Jacks advised, and

for a strange reason it was his mundane request that caused Cassandra to burst out crying, her body racked with great sobs as the stress and fears of the last twenty minutes found an outlet in the tears that ran unbidden down her chalk-white cheeks.

'That's it,' Jacks said coaxingly. 'Let it all out. You did well to keep it in for so long but it's time now to let the tears flow.'

'And you?' Cassandra questioned, in a broken, sob-racked voice. 'You've just killed four men and here you are driving along as though you had just stopped off for a coffee. What kind of man are you?'

'You just answered your own question,' Jacks came back, as he turned off the road and drove into a wooded area. 'I'm the kind of man who can kill four men then drive away as if I had just stopped off for a coffee. I'm the kind of man you need right now; without my famous ruthlessness we'd both already be dead. We're agreed that any one of the four men would have killed us given the chance?'

'Oh, I understand why you killed them,' Cassandra conceded, looking at Jacks through tear-brimmed eyes. 'It's your lack of reaction to doing so that confuses me. It was the same with the three you killed in the garage. Seven men dead and there's not even a tremor in your voice, no sign of nerves whatsoever.'

'It's just practised control,' Jacks explained. 'If you could see inside me, you'd be reading a different man. Inside I have to deal with a hundred reactions, but they're mine to deal with and I deal with them in my fashion. It's out of order you turning on me because I'm not shedding a tear. Perhaps I cried myself out a long, long time ago and have no tears left to shed.'

'I'm not turning on you,' Cassandra said softly. 'I could never do that; I just wish you would share the man inside with me.'

'You wouldn't know what to do with him,' Jacks replied. 'Simply because he wouldn't let you. Now, dry your tears. It's getting late and we need to find a bed for the night. It's either that or we sleep in the car. Are you with me?'

'I'm with you,' Cassandra said sincerely. 'But not in the way I would like to be.'

Jacks let it go at that.

★　★　★

When the elderly gentleman in the café returned to his Citroën, he found the bodies of the two dead assassins lying in pools of blood. As an ex-Paratrooper, he had seen his share of death, but even he was taken aback by his discovery and, as he hurried back into the café in order to call the police, he reflected on the fact that in life we are so often in the midst of death.

The local police arrived within five minutes and quickly turned the car-park into a crime scene. The dropped Heckler and Koch handguns by the bodies told their own story and when the second pair of bodies was discovered in the ladies toilet the story grew to the extent that the inspector in charge contacted the SDCE, the French secret service, who told him to seal the whole area, to take witness statements and then not to touch a thing until they got there.

A half-hour or so later, two helicopters landed in an adjacent field and very quickly the service station was swarming with forensic experts, photographers and serious-faced men in raincoats.

One of the policemen first on the scene had already phoned a man on the local paper who then called his contact at CNN and when they arrived with their satellite vans and cameras they found a very aggressive SDCE inspector known as Lafarge who threatened them with arrest if they interfered with his investigation. He promised them a statement later but for now he just told them to stay out of his way.

Earlier that afternoon, Lafarge had received a courtesy call from Jacob in London letting him know that Cassandra von Deker would be crossing his domain under the protection of Mister Jacks and he reasoned that the man and woman identified by the counter assistant had to be them. But even if he had no prior knowledge of Jacks being on his territory, Lafarge would have recognized his handiwork. Within the world's security services, Jacks was a bit of a legend. In this time of sophisticated weaponry, Jacks favoured using an Ivor Johnson, a .22 calibre weapon that carried only five bullets. Jacks always went for the difficult headshot and, judging by the entry wounds on the four bodies, they had been killed by small calibre bullets carrying explosive heads. The way Lafarge read the crime scene, Jacks had used the Deker woman to lure the first two assassins into the Ladies toilet where he killed them then, probably by mischance, he had encountered the second two in the carpark where he had killed them. All four assassins had been carrying 9mm Heckler and Koch USP9s and none of the four had got off a shot. The H&Ks were each holding a full clip which meant it had been a case of sixty bullets versus five. Putting this with the knowledge that only the evening before Jacks had killed three members of al-Hashashin in London, Lafarge was coming to believe that all the stories he had heard about him were true.

The dead assassins were fingerprinted and photographed and then with help from a computer network they were each identified as being members of al-Hashashin with connections to al-Qaeda, and Lafarge concluded his investigations by considering that Mister Jacks had done France a great service by ridding the land of them.

Two mobile phones and a laptop computer were found in the black BMWs and, within half an hour, they had been unlocked by experts to disclose the whereabouts of al-Hashashin/al-Qaeda headquarters in Paris and in Marseilles.

The local police had put out a call for a couple, believed to be English, travelling in a black Ford and Lafarge told the inspector in charge to cancel the call on the grounds that this was an anti-terrorist operation and that the couple worked for SDCE.

When the eight boisterous youths in the café were allowed to leave, the burger bag was discovered where a Transit van had been parked. On investigation, the sergeant who found it took it to Lafarge who, judging by the singed holes on the bottom together with the inside smell of cordite, surmised that it had been used by Jacks as an improvised silencer and he smiled at the thought of shooting someone through a couple of cheeseburgers, a device that rather made the case for fast food being a killer.

★ ★ ★

Twenty minutes after the police got to the service station, having been delayed by a bad traffic accident *en route*, two more members of al-Hashashin arrived on site. They had been summoned there with the news that Mister Jacks and the Deker woman were sitting in the café drinking coffee. Since then, they had been unable to contact anyone and when they saw the police cordon around the service station they thought they now knew why. By-passing the café area, they pulled into the petrol station and while one filled the car, the other gleaned information from the small crowd who had gathered to witness what was going on across the way.

The story was that four men had been shot and killed and that the car-park was awash with blood. The one filling the car was told a similar story by a garage attendant and the two assassins could only reason that the four men referred to were their brothers-in-arms. They each knew the four men as friends who had originally met at the same Lebanese training camp. The four were trained assassins and it was a mystery to them how

Jacks could have taken out all four. Surely no one was that good that they could take out four men armed with Heckler and Kochs, particularly when they knew that Jacks carried a small calibre weapon. Only yesterday, Jacks had killed three of their men in London and, like Cassandra, they came to wonder just what kind of man he was.

As they pondered on what next to do, the two helicopters landed in the adjacent field and when they saw men wearing body armour wielding Uzis in the company of men in suits and raincoats, they recognized them as SDCE and decided that the wise thing was to get as far away from the service station as they could.

A few miles on, one of the men used a mobile to contact headquarters and then delivered the bad news.

★   ★   ★

Back at CIA headquarters in London, Special Agent Grant was smiling to himself as he contacted Majors in Langley. 'Our boy's been very busy,' he said by way of greeting. 'He turned La Capelle into a battlefield.'

'According to CNN,' Majors came back, 'it was the work of the SDCE.'

'Pay no attention to that,' Grant stated.

139

'Our boy did the job. I think Lafarge is covering for him while capitalizing on the situation. Lafarge has a history with the Fox; he was probably well informed before the event.'

'Sounds reasonable,' Majors agreed. 'Do we know where Jacks is now?'

'Somewhere on the Belgium-Luxemburg border,' Grant replied. 'He'll spend the night somewhere and then tomorrow is the big day.'

'They'll be expecting him,' Majors stated.

'So are we,' Grant reminded. 'We and our Israeli friends have people on the ground to supply back-up and they're all hoping that Hitchcock turns up, we all have reasons for wanting to see him dead. The only drawback there is that no one knows what he looks like, least of all Jacks.'

'And it's highly unlikely that Azrael, that self-fashioned Angel of Death knows what Jacks looks like.' Majors commented.

'Two anonymous faceless men,' Grant mused. 'If it does go down then it will prove a very interesting confrontation. My money's still on our boy. The way he's been performing he makes the rest of us look like amateurs.'

'I suspect the opposite is true,' Majors responded. 'We're the professionals and Jacks is the amateur. We were trained to do what we do, and we do it from a sense of duty. Nobody ever trained Jacks and duty doesn't come into things. He's natural born and I suspect that he does what he does merely for the love of doing it.'

'You could be right there,' Grant conceded.

★   ★   ★

In the basement of the al-Hashashin base in Watford, England, on hearing the bad news from France, Rimmon felt like a man who had been hit on the back of the head with a hammer. The last he heard was that two members of the assassination squad had Jacks and the woman cornered in a service station café just outside La Capelle and that the other four members of the squad were *en route* there. So how had four of them ended up dead in the car-park?

Not that it really mattered how Jacks had accomplished the feat, fact was he had killed the four men and in doing so, Rimmon thought that he might as well have killed him while he was at it because that was what he had done.

Any minute now, Rimmon was expecting to hear that he was being replaced and to be summoned back to the Lebanon. Come the end, al-Hashashin was an unforgiving organization and he decided that he would do the honourable thing by killing himself. In doing so, he would be probably be denied entry to Paradise but he hoped that his sacrifice would excuse his great shame.

Perhaps Allah would be forgiving.

★   ★   ★

Azrael had been out scouting the area around the Luxemburg bank. On returning to his hotel room, he found a message waiting for him on his laptop. When he had fully digested the contents of the message, he was left a man swamped by disbelief. A six-man squad had gone after Jacks and he had somehow managed to leave four dead in a car-park while the other two had fled the scene when the French security force showed up. How had Jacks managed to kill four of the best? Azrael did not personally know any of the assassination squad, but as members of al-Hashashin they were highly trained in weaponry. So, how had Jacks succeeded in getting the drop on all four?

As things stood, Jacks and the woman now had a clear run to Luxemburg and Azrael knew he would need to be ready for him when he got there, very ready indeed. He had been given a three man back-up team, armed with long guns. Initially, known as one who ever worked alone, pride made him reluctant to accept the men. But now he was glad they were there. He would instruct them only to shoot Cassandra von Deker; with her death the contract with al-Qaeda would be honoured. After that, Jacks would be his to deal with and he rested secure in the knowledge that he had a double edge over Jacks. Jacks did not know what he looked like, but he knew what Cassandra von Deker looked like and where the woman went so would Jacks be at her side.

The other side of the edge was more subtle, but it could be the one that made the difference. Considering the assassins that Jacks had already encountered and his likely preconceived concepts of terrorists, Jacks was almost certain to be checking the crowded streets in search of an Arabic face and though Muslim to his soul, Azrael could never be mistaken as an Arab.

★   ★   ★

What Azrael did not know was that his three man back-up squad had already been spotted by sundry CIA and MOSSAD agents and were there to be taken when the time came.

The agents did not spot Azrael simply because he had driven into the country from France and registered in the Luxemburg hotel using his real name, a name supported by a genuine British passport.

13

As Jacks drove through the darkness, he reflected on the fact that the journey from Calais had taken him around and across some of the most infamous battlefields in the world's history. Here he was now on the fringe of the Ardennes, a place the Americans thought impenetrable, but through which the German Army rode 600 Tiger tanks. He was on the verge of voicing his thoughts but decided that this perhaps was not the time to engage Cassandra in a conversation revolving around warfare and its dead millions. Instead. he asked, 'Do you speak good French?'

'Swiss finishing school,' Cassandra said, by way of reply.

Jacks smiled into the night. 'Of course,' he said. 'So put your expensive education to use and switch on the radio. It's coming up for the hour; I'm afraid we might be headline news.'

Cassandra did as asked, tuned into a station and then listened intently to the first news report. Beside her, Jacks picked out the odd word, three references to the French security services, but without Cassandra there to translate his interpretation would have been a long way out.

'According to the news,' Cassandra said excitedly, 'the SDCE earlier conducted an anti-terrorist raid that resulted in the deaths of four armed terrorists. The incident took place at a roadside café just south of La Capelle . . . what does it mean?'

'It means that we now don't have to worry about the Gendarmes being on our trail,' Jacks replied. 'It means that for reasons of their own, the SDCE is shielding us while capitalizing on the situation. My friend back in London has strong connections with French security; they probably knew in advance that we were crossing their territory. As a pal of mine would say — what a result.'

'Doesn't it concern you that they're taking the credit for something you alone did?' Cassandra asked rather naïvely.

Jacks shook his head in disbelief. 'Do you really think that I want to be credited with killing four men?' he asked shortly. 'The French have done me a service. Without their shield, right now we would probably be the two most wanted in the country and we have enough to be going on with without having Inspector Clouseau hunting us down.'

Cassandra smiled at the image that formed in her mind.

'Good to see you smile again,' Jacks said sincerely. 'With no police on our backs I think we can take a chance on a hotel. So keep your eyes peeled. I don't know about you but I'm starving. And I need a shower; I have that smell of death about me.'

Inside, Cassandra flinched at Jacks's words but, at the same time, the prospect of spending the night alone with him in a hotel excited her.

In the hope of eventually reaching the Belgium-Luxemburg border, Jacks had made a couple of right turns and when he made a third, he caught a glimpse of what he took to be a large house and thinking it might be a hotel, he turned through a pair of open metal gates on to a driveway that led to a building he quickly recognized as being a little more than a mere house.

'It's a privately owned château,' Cassandra said, as Jacks brought the Ford to a stop. 'We'd better turn around.'

'I'm not very good at turning around,' Jacks replied, as he switched off the engine and opened his door and got out of the car. 'While we're here we may as well give them a knock.'

'Whatever are you going to say to whoever answers?' Cassandra asked, as she got out her side, somewhat intrigued by her situation.

'That depends on who answers my knock,'

147

Jacks replied, as they walked side by side to the front door, an ornate oak affair that boasted a family crest as a doorknocker.

Jacob once said of Jacks that he would eat when the crows were starving. But it was not just that Jacks was a mere survivor. There are two kinds of survivor, the practical kind like Robinson Crusoe, and the lucky kind like Ulysses. Jacks believed that he was cut from the mould of the latter. Had Jacks been Robinson Crusoe, he would not have met Man Friday, he would have met Woman Sunday and she would have turned out to be the king's only daughter. Jacks believed in his luck and it had been a while since he had called upon it to get him out of a hole and, as he knocked on the château door, he was hoping that it had not deserted him.

Things got off to a bad start when his knock was answered by a butler wearing a striped waistcoat and a look about him that told Jacks he had seen more in life than the bottom of a kitchen sink. The butler gave them a suspicious look then informed them that the marchioness was not receiving visitors.

Jacks understood enough of the French and said to Cassandra, 'Tell him to tell the marchioness that we are not visitors. We seek sanctuary. It's a case of *noblesse oblige.*'

The way the butler raised an eyebrow told

Jacks that he understood English, but he listened politely to Cassandra's exact translation before closing the door and departing to deliver the message.

'You ever notice,' Jacks observed, 'how doormen do what they are told from both sides of the door?'

Cassandra hadn't but she did not say so; instead she asked, 'Do you think they'll let us in?'

'What marchioness worth her coronet could resist a call of *noblesse oblige*?' Jacks answered, as the door was opened and the butler invited them in, closed the door and then led them into a huge living-room centred by a fire that roared in a grate contained by a huge, ornate mantel. The furniture was period French and Jacks smiled as the most beautiful woman he had seen in a long time rose from a splendid armchair.

'I am the Marchioness de Thionville,' she said in English. 'Ronald tells me you seek sanctuary. May I learn from whom or from what?' She asked the question of both of them but it was Jacks she looked at.

'Assassins,' Jacks answered. 'There are people trying to kill us.'

The marchioness raised a slim hand to an elegant throat and said, 'Then you had best sit down.'

Jacks was smiling as he made himself comfortable on a chair, leaving Cassandra to perch on the edge of a couch that was so big it made her feel small. As the marchioness saw Cassandra in profile, she nodded to herself and said, 'I know you. You're Cassandra von Deker. Your picture has been all over the press but I not only recognize you from the front pages, my father knew your father. I once spent some time at your lodge in the Black Forest.'

'I don't remember ever meeting you,' Cassandra said, not at all liking the way the other woman was looking at Jacks.

'I think you were at school somewhere,' the marchioness said factually while making it sound like Cassandra was a mere child. 'And now that I know who the young lady is,' she went on, looking boldly at Jacks, 'perhaps I can learn who you are?'

Jacks held her look while telling Cassandra to tell her who he was, doing so because he was curious as to how she would describe him with another woman listening in.

Cassandra raised her head and looked the beautiful Marchioness de Thionville in the face. 'His name is Mister Jacks; he's my guardian,' she began in an apparent possessive tone. 'He's my protector; he's my lifesaver. My angel with black wings.'

The marchioness knew then that Cassandra was in love with the man with the intense eyes, but she also knew that where the man may be her lifesaver he held no such affection for her. 'Does she describe you well?' she asked, returning her interested eyes back on Jacks.

'If that's how she sees me,' Jacks replied, with eyes just as interested. 'Then that's how she sees me. A bit poetic at the end but she paints a fair image. And what's your name?'

'Gabriella,' the marchioness replied without hesitation. 'But tell me this, if you are a bodyguard, does that mean that there is now a gun under my roof?'

Jacks shook his head. 'There are now *two* guns under your roof,' he corrected. 'I have one inside my coat and Cassandra here has a .45 automatic tucked away inside her bag. But they're no threat to you,' he went on, all the time reading the obvious message that Gabriella was transmitting by way of her grey, limpid eyes. 'You want us to leave, we go with a fond farewell.'

Gabriella smiled. 'I am no stranger to guns,' she said, looking at Jacks. 'You are my guests; I offer you sanctuary,' she went on, as she pressed a bell by the fireplace. 'Shall you be requiring one room or two?'

The question was asked directly of Jacks

and he was smiling as he said that two would be needed.

When the butler appeared, Gabriella instructed him to show the young lady to the White Room and the gentleman to the Red. 'I'm sorry they're so far apart,' she said, looking from Jacks to Cassandra then back again, 'But they're the only two guest rooms with *en suite* bathrooms. Do you have any luggage?'

'In the car,' Jacks replied.

'Ronald will collect it for you,' Gabriella responded.

'No he won't,' Jacks said, as he got to his feet. 'I'll collect it for myself,' he concluded, as he signalled to Cassandra to get to her feet. 'We appreciate this,' he went on, giving Gabriella the same look as she was giving him. 'We truly do.'

Gabriella smiled a smile she had not smiled in a long time, and when she did the woman shone from within her. 'It is my pleasure,' she replied sincerely. 'Are you hungry?'

Gabriella's question was ambiguous in that it left open what Jacks might be hungry for. 'When it gets to food,' he answered, 'I always seem to be hungry . . . but tonight I have developed a particular appetite.'

Gabriella almost blushed. 'I'm sure we can find something to your taste,' she said in a voice gone somewhat husky.

Jacks only smiled, but as Cassandra followed him and the butler out of the room she looked sulky. The night was not going as she had thought and hoped it might. She had known from the minute she heard that there was a marchioness in residence that something was going to spoil her plans. She had been hoping that she would turn out to be a hundred years old but of course, she hadn't. She turned out to be the beautiful, elegant, sophisticated bitch she was. She'd been flirting with her protector since first she laid eyes on him and, what was worse, he had responded in kind. How could he be so insensitive to her feelings that he could sit there in front of her seducing another woman with his eyes? Did he truly not care about her at all?

The bitch had been holding all the trump cards, sitting there in her designer dress, not a hair out of place, looking like she'd just stepped out of a fashion magazine while she'd been sitting there, dressed by Oxfam, not a hair *in* place, looking like she'd just stepped out of a muddy puddle. Life was not fair, it really wasn't!

When Jacks retrieved the luggage from the boot of the Ford Focus, he went to his survival box and extracted a slim leather belt holding fifteen of his special .22 bullets. After tonight, he only had one bullet left in his Ivor Johnson and the way al-Hashashin was performing, he doubted if one bullet would be enough to finish the job he had set out to do. On impulse and because he did not know how many curtained windows he might need to study, he also retrieved a small pair of powerful binoculars.

On returning to the hallway, Jacks handed Cassandra her valise and the way she snatched it out of his hand told him that he had done something to upset her . . . again. Curious to learn what major crime he had committed this time, he waited until the butler had opened the door to the White Room then asked her.

'You know,' she said accusingly, as she marched into a delicate, pastel room dominated by a wider than usual single bed. 'Have you no feelings at all?'

Here we go, Jacks thought. What was it with the female of the species that made them bring feelings and emotion into everything? As he only had a vague idea of what these concepts meant, he often ended up thinking he was missing something. 'I hold a certain affection for a cat called Rambo,' he replied, as the butler's responsive laugh that hid behind a phoney cough betrayed again the

154

fact that he understood English.

'You're infuriating!' Cassandra almost spat. 'The most infuriating man I have ever met.'

'In relation to whom?' a smiling Jacks asked, just to further infuriate her and then beat a hasty retreat out into the corridor before she did the womanly thing and started throwing things at him.

The butler backed out of the doorway and, as Cassandra slammed it shut, he gave Jacks a look of one man speaking to another then led him further down a corridor, around a corner before stopping and opening a door that led into a bedroom. 'The Red Room,' he announced in English. 'You'll find all you might need in the bathroom.'

'A Tiger tank?' Jacks questioned with a grin.

The butler smiled back.

14

Once inside the Red Room, Jacks went directly into the *en suite* bathroom, turned on the shower, hurriedly undressed then stepped under the flow of hot water as though stepping under the Fountain of Youth, revitalizing himself as he scrubbed away the smell of death he believed he carried with him.

Jacks spent a good ten minutes cleansing himself and when he returned to the bedroom, a towel wrapped round his waist, he was feeling lighter in body and in spirit. Being Mister Jacks put a lot of pressure on his soul.

His mind at rest, he sat on the large double bed and used his cloned mobile phone to contact Jacob back in London. As ever, he answered immediately and Jacks smiled to hear the genuine concern in his voice when he asked if he was safe.

'Pretty much safe for the night,' Jacks replied. 'You know how lucky I can be? Well, tonight the Fates have been really kind. You'll be up to date with La Capelle? What's going on with the SDCE?'

'Right now,' Jacob replied, 'you're their favourite person. They found two BMWs at Capelle just full of information. I've not long spoken with my counterpart in France and he informs me that the information gathered led to two raids on houses in Paris and one in Marseilles. Three further terrorists were killed, bomb-making equipment was found, along with a wealth of information that will be an aid to every anti-terrorist group in the world. The story is about to break. By tomorrow morning La Capelle and the follow ups will be on the front page around the world.'

'Well,' Jacks drawled. 'There's a thing! Just so long as I don't get a mention.'

'You won't, I guarantee that,' Jacob stated. 'The Americans are particularly pleased. One of the terrorists killed in Paris was one of the three men who escaped with Omar al-Farouk from their supposedly secure detention centre at Bagram airbase. British Special Forces killed al-Farouk in Basra and now the French have captured one. You may have inadvertently helped patch up US-Franco relations.'

'So now I'm a diplomat?' Jacks asked drily.

Jacob chuckled. 'That'll be the day!' he said just as drily. 'Where are you?'

'Somewhere near the Luxemburg border,' Jacks replied. 'At least I hope I am. I might have got lost in the woods. I'll find out later from mine host exactly where I'm spending the night.'

'You're in a hotel?'

'A château,' Jacks corrected.

'A château?' Jacob questioned admiringly. 'And does it come complete with the mandatory countess in exile?'

'Marchioness,' Jacks said with a smile. 'Beautiful as they make them but, more than that, I think she'll prove useful when it gets to me delivering Cassandra to the bank. The enemy knows what car I'm driving, so I'm hoping to borrow one here. You know me, Jacob, the job comes first.'

'I have some news on Luxemburg,' Jacob responded. 'The people on the ground there have identified three probable and two possible. They'll be taken out of things when the time is right. I did tell you that you would have support waiting for you.'

'So you did,' Jacks agreed. 'That's a big help and you know me, I need all the help I can get.'

'There's more,' Jacob said. 'The people on the ground are hoping that one of the five suspects turns out to be Azrael, the one the CIA calls Hitchcock, but I know from the descriptions of the men that they don't have Azrael in their net.'

'And how do you know that?' Jacks asked, as a certain hope was born.

'Remember Goldstein?' Jacob began in reply. 'As he always does, Azrael filmed the assassination and earlier tonight it was broadcast on the Internet. My people studied it and found what they thought at first was a smear that ran for four seconds before the film started. On studying the smear, and by doing the remarkable things these people can do, they eventually learned that the smear was in fact a moving shot of a man's lower face, lips down to chin. For those four seconds the camera lens was focused backwards. I can tell you that Azrael is clean-shaven, he has a definite cleft in his chin, he is thin-lipped and, best of all, he's not Arabic, he's Caucasian.'

'You mean he's white?' Jacks asked bluntly.

'He is,' Jacob confirmed. 'And a couple of other things. The bit of stubble beneath his bottom lip suggests he has fair, possibly even ginger hair and, by the angle of the shot, my people are eighty per cent certain that the camera was held in the right hand . . . '

'Which would make Azrael left-handed,' Jacks finished, suddenly feeling as though a great weight had been lifted from his mind. 'You've served me well here, Jacob. I now know who *not* to look out for. With your information, I now have the edge. Have you passed this on to the people on the ground?'

'Not yet.'

'Don't,' Jacks asked. 'If he's there, I want him. The others were just self-defence; him I don't like. He makes a mockery out of death.'

'He could probably be taken out of the picture,' Jacob reminded.

'I know,' Jacks conceded. 'But I'd prefer to take him out myself.'

'As you wish,' Jacob granted.

The call ended by Jacob wishing Jacks *bon chance* leaving him in a much better frame of mind than he had been in before making the call. All the time while conversing with Cassandra and Gabriella, a corner of his mind had been working on the problem of tomorrow. He had imagined any number of assassins lying in wait around the Luxemburg bank but, the way it was looking now, he could end up with having only one to deal with. Perhaps, after all, a single bullet would be enough.

With such thoughts, Jacks got dressed, loaded the Ivor Johnson then stuck it in his trouser belt underneath his overhanging shirt. He had considered leaving the gun behind, but not only would he feel naked without it but it would be downright disrespectful of him to leave behind a loyal friend who had served him well over the years.

From there, hoping to find her in a friendlier frame of mind, Jacks went to call Cassandra for dinner.

After a shower, a change of clothes, with a touch of make-up and her hair in place, Cassandra too was in a much better frame of mind. She was still angry with Jacks for flirting with the marchioness but she had convinced herself that flirting with her did not mean he would follow through. Flirting was one thing, but she could not imagine any man, not even Jacks, having the audacity to sleep with another woman while in her company. Her reasoning was quite sound, but there was a little voice in her head that kept reminding her that Jacks was a different kind of man and that if any man was capable of such audacity, then that man was him.

But surely he would not be so cruel.

When Jacks knocked on her door she opened it with a welcoming smile and said, 'At last, if I don't eat soon, I think I'll faint,' and then, patting the obvious gun at Jacks's waist, she asked mischievously if she should bring along her .45.

Jacks grinned widely. 'Surely you don't want to shoot our hostess?' he enquired, as Cassandra took his offered left arm.

'Now, why would I want to do a thing like

161

that?' Cassandra asked innocently.

'You have me there,' Jacks said, and he was not speaking lightly.

★ ★ ★

When Jacks and Cassandra reached the bottom of the grand staircase, Gabriella appeared in a lighted doorway and invited them to come in. A fire roared in an open grate while a solitary chandelier lit the end of a highly polished table that had been laid for three. 'You sit here,' she said, placing Jacks at the head of the table, Cassandra to his left while she chose to sit to his right. 'I wonder what Ronald has concocted for us,' she mused.

I wonder what you are concocting, Cassandra thought, smiling as Gabriella's eyebrows rose to see Jacks place a gun on the table. 'He always brings Mr Ivor Johnson to dinner,' she said, hoping to score points on the bitch sitting opposite who somehow looked even more beautiful than she had earlier. 'I asked him if I should bring my .45 but he assured me that I would have no need of it.'

Gabriella smiled for Cassandra then turned to Jacks and said, 'An Ivor Johnson? That's a marksman's pistol, isn't it?'

Gabriella's knowledge floored Cassandra while impressing Jacks. 'You know your guns,' he said.

'My husband knew them,' Gabriella corrected. 'I learned from him. I recognized it by the owl-head stamp on the butt.'

Ronald chose that moment to enter and the trio watched in silence as he wheeled a trolley to the side of the table and laid a steaming plate first in front of Gabriella, then Cassandra. When he laid a similar plate in front of Jacks and he saw a bed of rice, some kind of fish or other covered in a sauce predominately pink in colour, he was not sure if he was hungry enough to take it on. One mouthful changed his mind, and was quickly followed by a second, then a third, until he became aware that he was shovelling the food into his mouth. Catching Cassandra looking at him disapprovingly, he stopped eating long enough to say, 'I'd like to blame it on my hunger, or on the delicious taste but, truth is, I'm just a savage at heart.'

Gabriella laughed and her dulcet tone cut through Cassandra like a chain saw. God, the bitch was so perfect, she thought, as she poured herself a large glass of white wine. Gabriella let her glass be half filled and when she saw Cassandra put the bottle down, ignoring the third glass, she threw her a questioning look.

Cassandra downed half her glass of wine, threw Gabriella back a challenging look and said, with a hint of sarcasm, 'Mister Jacks doesn't drink alcohol. He says it dulls the senses,' she went on, draining her glass. 'And that it's bad for the soul.'

Recognizing petulance when they saw it, Jacks and Gabriella exchanged a knowing smile. 'It's nice to be quoted,' Jacks said, shaking his head at Cassandra as she poured herself more wine. 'And nice to see you're paying no attention to my warnings. I love a rebel, don't you, Gabriella?'

Feeling a tinge of sympathy for Cassandra, Gabriella settled for a smile as an answer.

The disapproving look Jacks gave her had Cassandra feeling like the little girl out of her depth in adult company, just as she used to feel whenever she had dinner with her parents. 'I'm sorry,' she said, as she had said many times back then.

'What's to be sorry about?' Jacks questioned shortly, as he finished his meal. 'Come on, enjoy all this,' he said, waving an arm round the room. 'Were we lucky, or were we lucky?'

Cassandra read that to mean that it was *he* who had been lucky, where she'd just been dragged along like a piece of luggage, but she was not drunk enough to say so and from there she resolved to say no more.

'That was delicious,' Jacks said, as he pushed away his empty plate. 'What's the story on Ronald? Does he come with the family?'

'It's not my family,' Gabriella said, as Jacks appreciated the way she used a pink-tipped tongue to remove a fleck of fish from a full bottom lip. 'My husband was the marquis. I married the title. I was judged to have married above my station, Charles's family are none too fond of me.'

'There's a family in New York has the same attitude to me,' Jacks said with a big smile. 'They're called the Corleones.'

Gabriella knew the reference and got the joke; Cassandra thought Jacks was being serious and missed it. When Gabriella laughed again and Jacks laughed with her, she felt so left out of things, her heart despaired.

'Ronald came with my husband's family,' Gabriella went on, talking as though Cassandra was not there. 'He grew with Charles and along the way learned from the master chefs of Europe. When Charles followed the family tradition and went into the military, Ronald went along as his batman.'

'St Cyr?' Jacks asked.

Gabriella nodded. 'And then on into the regular army before being promoted and transferred to the Legion.'

Jacks was impressed. 'The French Foreign Legion is up there with the best in the world,' he stated sincerely. 'Dien Bien Phu was one of the greatest stands in history . . . did your husband die in the field?'

'Tragically no,' Gabriella replied, as a certain sadness shifted across her pearl-grey eyes. 'He had a love of fast cars and one day he drove one just that bit *too* fast. The family ignored me at his funeral and Ronald and I were left to share our grief. He has been with me ever since. I don't like driving and he gets me to where I want to go and, as you have tasted, he's a marvellous cook.'

'Gordon Blue himself,' Jacks said.

Gabriella smiled. 'He's a master with sauces but he excels as a pâtissier. I've asked him to prepare something suitably tasty,' she concluded, as Jacks smiled to feel a shoeless foot rest on his right ankle.

'After the piquant sauce on the salmon,' Jacks responded. 'I could just eat something hot and sweet.'

For the second time that night, Gabriella almost blushed while Cassandra seethed.

The something tasty prepared by Ronald turned out to be an almond slice, a particular favourite of Jacks's but where he must have eaten a thousand varieties over the years, he had to own that he had never before eaten a pastry quite as succulent as the one that just melted in his mouth. 'Outstanding,' he declared. 'If my mum had cooked like Ronald, I never would have run away from home . . . Did you enjoy yours, Cassandra?'

'I wish I had room for more,' Cassandra replied, slightly slurring her words.

'Did you truly run away from home?' Gabriella asked, with a hint of concern.

'I ran away from somewhere,' Jacks qualified. 'But home is not the word. Best move I ever made. Look what it's led me to, dining in a château with a pretty girl and a beautiful woman. It's times like this that make living worthwhile . . . but tomorrow is going to be a different day,' he continued, looking at Gabriella. 'Tomorrow Cassandra and I have to visit a certain bank in Luxemburg. The people trying to kill us will be waiting and, as they know what car I'm driving, I was wondering if I could borrow one from you.'

'Charles not only drove fast cars,' Gabriella responded, 'He collected them. There are four in the garage. In the morning, you can take your pick. They're all in good running order; Ronald takes them out for a run regularly.'

'First class,' Jacks announced, smiling only for Gabriella. 'You're golden, that's what you are. When the job is done in Luxemburg, I'll drive it back here and pick up the Ford.'

Cassandra did not at all like the sound of that, but Gabriella smiled at the prospect while being impressed with Jacks's self-confidence. 'Tell me,' she asked, 'earlier when I asked you from whom you needed sanctuary and you referred to assassins, were you speaking in general terms, or were you referring to *Les Assassins*, al-Qaeda's personal killers?'

'You did learn a lot from your husband,' Jacks said respectfully. 'Al-Hashashin or *Les Assassins* — they're not very nice people.'

Gabriella nodded in agreement. 'Now tell me this,' she continued, soft eyes on Jacks. 'On your journey to my door, did you perchance stop off for a coffee near a place called La Capelle?'

Jacks smiled. 'Did we, Cassandra?' he asked in reply.

'We stopped off somewhere, but I'm not sure where,' Cassandra replied, happy to be united with Jacks in the face of this prying bitch. 'Why do you ask?'

'La Capelle is all over the news,' Gabriella answered. 'There was an incident there earlier tonight involving the SDCE and four dead armed terrorists. First reports said that the police wanted to speak with a couple, believed to be English, who were seen driving off in a dark Ford. They haven't been mentioned since and I was just wondering.'

'It looks like we missed all the action, Cassandra,' Jacks said, while looking at Gabriella. 'Perhaps we should have hung on for a second coffee. We heard something on the car radio and according to what we heard it was an SDCE anti-terrorist situation. Surely you don't think I might have killed four men all by my lonesome? I'm good, but I'm not that good. Now you tell me something. Where exactly am I?'

'A few miles north of Longuyon,' Gabriella replied, as she noted how neatly Jacks had changed the subject. 'Not far from the Luxemburg border.

'How far to Luxemburg itself?'

'A hundred and fifty kilometres give or take.'

'A couple of hours away,' Jacks said with a hint of relief. 'The way I've been driving I could have been near Berlin.'

The heat from the dying fire behind her, the heady wine, the rich food finally caught up with Cassandra as her body gave up fighting tiredness and spoke up for itself with a yawn.

Jacks read Cassandra's yawn as a cue and announced that he too was tired. It had been a long day and tomorrow could prove even longer.

15

With Cassandra a little unsteady on her legs, Jacks supported her upstairs to her allocated room. When he opened the door for her, he said, 'Get a good night's sleep and don't worry. I'll see you through whatever lies ahead. By this time tomorrow all this will just be a memory. You'll have your old life back.'

'What if I don't want all this to be over;' Cassandra asked, squeezing Jack's arm tightly. 'What if I don't want my old life back?'

'One way or another tomorrow will see the end of this,' Jacks stated, as he extricated himself from her grip. 'After that, your life's yours to do what you want with. For now, just go to bed. I'll knock when it's time to start moving.'

'You won't come in?' she asked, almost hating herself for being so weak as to ask.

'Cassandra,' Jacks said, with a disapproving shake of his head, 'you really should not drink. I'm going to bed,' he stated, 'before you feel foolish.'

So saying, Jacks turned away and walked off down the dimly lit corridor without a backward glance. Cassandra watched him until he disappeared around a corner, quietly shut her door, before throwing herself on the bed and having a quiet sob. Self-pity had long been a refuge of hers, but this time she came to see the hopelessness of such an attitude, eventually snapping herself out of her threatening depression by resolving to press on regardless. Could Jacks ever love a woman who indulged in self-pity? With him her only hope was to be strong and to look to the future.

With such thoughts, Cassandra got off the bed and went into the *en suite* bathroom where she washed her face, flinching at the sight of her red eyes and tearstained cheeks, then changed into her favourite nightie. When she got into bed, as exhausted as she was, she thought sleep would come quickly, but her imaginings held Morpheus at bay for quite a while. She just knew that Gabriella would visit Jacks in the night and the thought of them being together was as embarrassing to her as it was disturbing.

But Morpheus has his subtle ways and, eventually, he captured her in his arms and transported her to the realm of dreams.

★ ★ ★

The next thing Cassandra knew, she was coming awake to the sound of someone knocking and calling her name. When she realized that it was Jacks who was summoning her, she came instantly awake, sat up in bed and told him to come in.

Jacks entered bearing a tray and what looked like a black dress draped over an arm. 'Happy Birthday,' he said, laying the tray before her to reveal poached eggs on toast, a cup of coffee set beside a small bowl of multi-coloured flowers. 'I'd sing to you,' he went on, as he drew open a set of curtains, 'but, believe me, you should be glad that I don't. Did you sleep well?'

Cassandra thought that being woken by Jacks was like being woken by a tornado and it took her a couple of minutes to adjust to his pace. 'Thank you for the flowers,' she said, and then noticed that Jacks was wearing a uniform. 'Why are you dressed as a chauffeur?' she wanted to know.

'Plans have changed,' Jacks replied, as he sat on the end of the bed. 'Gabriella has increased her offer. The plan now is that we use the Rolls Royce, I play the chauffeur, you play the maid, and Gabriella plays the marchioness. Here's your costume,' he concluded, laying the black dress on the bed.

'You want me to dress as a maid?'

Cassandra breathed.

'If I can put this outfit on, then you can dress as Coco the Clown,' Jacks responded. 'I've told Gabriella about the possible dangers, but she's determined to help.'

'I bet she is,' Cassandra said coldly.

Jacks was somewhat taken aback by the venom in Cassandra's tone. 'Whatever do you mean?' he wanted to know.

'I mean that she'd do anything to stay close to you,' Cassandra stated. 'You slept with her, didn't you?' she said accusingly.

'Cassandra,' Jacks said, with a warning tone, 'you're setting off down a road you have no right to walk down. Let it go.'

But Cassandra could not let go. 'I wasn't certain before,' she went on, 'but I am now; you did sleep with her, didn't you?'

'Oh, well,' Jacks sighed, in a resigned tone. 'If you must know, I did not so much sleep with Gabriella as she slept with me. Do you want to hear the ins and outs?'

Cassandra blushed. 'How could you?' she demanded to know.

'I could because I could,' he replied. 'I could because I wanted to. Now, why don't we move on; we have lots to prepare. And you haven't touched your breakfast.'

'I hate you,' Cassandra said, as she pushed her tray aside.

Jacks smiled. 'So much for being your hero,' he said, grinning wider. 'Looks like I have feet of clay. Come the end, I don't see what I get up to overnight as being any of your business.'

'But I love you,' Cassandra declared.

Mentally, Jacks took a backward step. 'I doubt that,' he stated. 'Infatuated perhaps, a bit overpowered by all the excitement; after all, it's not every day you meet a killer. Call it what you like, but love isn't the word.'

'Don't tell me how I feel,' Cassandra challenged. 'When I say I love you, it's because I do.'

'Do you mean you love me like you loved your mum and dad, like you loved your brother, your cat, your canary, designer dresses and, for all I know, cold rice pudding? I don't understand love. I'm sorry, but I don't.'

'You understood enough about it to let Gabriella into your bed,' Cassandra countered accusingly.

'Wait a minute,' Jacks said, as he raised his hands defensively. 'Gabriella had nothing to do with love, for where I know nothing about the noble sentiment, I know all about lust, passion and desire. Gabriella was a woman in need and, as I fed her hunger, she fed mine. Love didn't come into it. Like I told you, I don't understand love; it's part of my condition. A condition that has broken more than one woman's heart.'

'That's the second time you've mentioned your condition,' Cassandra said, feeling better to have learned that Jacks's encounter with Gabriella was just sex. 'Are you speaking in general terms, or does it have a recognizable name?'

'That depends on what school of thought you listen to,' Jacks answered with a smile. 'There's a man in a white coat who will tell you that I'm a controlled psychopath; there's one in a rumpled suit who'll tell you that I undoubtedly have a Multiple Personality Disorder; then there's my favourite, the man with the white hair who diagnosed Asperger Syndrome.'

'My brother knew an Aspergian,' Cassandra said thoughtfully. 'But he is nothing like you.'

'No two Aspergians are alike,' Jacks said informingly. 'At least, so they tell me. I don't really pay any attention to the labels people have hung round my neck. Asperger's Syndrome is named after the vain doctor who first diagnosed the condition; it could just as well be called Smith's Syndrome, or a thousand other names. And what's in a name, by any I'm just as complex. I know I'm different to other people, but I've come to live at peace with my difference. I'm just me and I like being the man I am.'

Cassandra should have let it go at that but there was one more thing she needed to know. 'What would you have done had I come to your bed?' she asked.

'Oh, Cassandra,' Jacks sighed in reply. 'You seem really intent on hurting yourself.'

'Tell me,' Cassandra insisted.

Jacks shrugged. 'I would have sent you back to your own bed,' he replied. 'And before you ask, not because I find you undesirable — the reverse is the truth. You're a very attractive girl, but if I let you into my bed then I would have to seduce you. Gabriella and I met on common ground; with you I would need to wander the fields of innocence. In seducing you I would need to capitalize on the misconceptions you have of me. As your hero, how could you deny me? I would end up feeling like a dirty old man who'd betrayed a sacred trust. Once before I corrupted innocence, and I came to find the inherent responsibilities unbearable.'

'You certainly know how to let a girl down gently,' Cassandra conceded with a genuine smile. 'But I'm not that innocent.'

'Believe me,' Jacks said from his heart, 'beside me, you are. If I seduced you, I would steal your heart then not know what to do with it . . . Now,' he continued, as he stood up, 'you need to get ready. Gabriella suggests you wear your hair up in a bun.'

'Oh, does she?' Cassandra questioned.

'Listen,' Jacks went on in a hard tone, 'I don't want any more of this childish nonsense about Gabriella. You're talking about the woman who gave us sanctuary, the woman who fed us and gave us shelter from the storm. A woman who is now prepared to help us even though she knows doing so could prove a threat to her life. You're twenty-one today, perhaps it's time you grew up and became the woman you claim to be.'

On his way out, Jacks collected the .45 from Cassandra's canvas bag. 'You won't be needing this,' he said, holding it aloft. 'But I might. Any time you're ready, we'll be waiting downstairs. Just bring your canvas bag, abandon the rest,' he concluded then left the room.

Cassandra felt as though she had just been slapped hard across the face, but, as she recalled what Jacks had said to her, she had to admit that he was right about Gabriella and that he was right about her needing to grow up. If she was ever to be seen favourably in his eyes then she had better do it fast.

In such a mind, Cassandra got out of bed,

showered quickly, dressed in the maid's dress and then did her hair up in a bun. When she went downstairs, carrying her canvas bag in one hand, breakfast tray in another, she wondered if real maids felt as self-conscious as she did. When she saw Gabriella, looking resplendent in a long, pearl-grey buttoned coat set off by a wide-brimmed dark-grey hat that matched her shoes, she went on to wonder if all maids envied their mistress.

'You're looking good,' Jacks said drily, but he smiled as he said it. 'Better than me, I don't know how I look but I feel somewhat foolish.'

'It's definitely not you,' Gabriella said with a smile. 'And a maid's outfit is certainly not you either, Cassandra. But isn't the whole idea that you look different than you really are?'

Cassandra smiled for Gabriella and said, 'But I still feel terribly self-conscious.'

'I always look different to what I really am,' Jacks said, smiling for all. 'Now, are we going to get out of here? We have an appointment at a bank in Luxemburg.'

Jacks was carrying a small valise that he gripped tightly as he played the chauffeur, holding the back door open for madam and her maid to enter, closing it when they were safely seated.

The Rolls was left-hand drive. When Jacks got behind the wheel, he laid the valise on the passenger seat, unzipped it, retrieved his Ivor Johnson from under his cashmere coat and put it between his legs, located the .45, put it within easy reach and then settled back, a man prepared to face whatever might lie ahead, a man ready to do whatever needed to be done.

Smiling at his reflection in the rear-view mirror, Jacks adjusted the peaked, chauffeur's hat so it sat more comfortably on his head, switched on the powerful engine and then pulled away from the château feeling very confident about the day.

It was certain that people would be waiting by the bank in Luxemburg, but where they would have imagined many ways he could arrive there was not a chance that they would imagine him pulling up directly in front of the bank in the company of a genuine marchioness and her maid while driving a cream Rolls Royce.

No chance whatsoever.

16

Ahead in Luxemburg City, as well as enemies, Jacks had unknown allies awaiting his arrival at the bank. The night before, while MOSSAD kept their usual low profile, the chief CIA agent on the ground informed the Luxemburg/Belgian authorities about what was going on in their beautiful city. As a rule, Inspector Javier would have greatly resented the CIA being on his territory, but in the war against terrorism, all allies were welcome.

Javier had read in the press about Cassandra von Deker's lucky escape in London but he had never imagined finding her under threat right here on his doorstep. The very thought of more assassins waiting to kill her infuriated his moral sensibilities and he resolved to protect her to the best of his resources. He began by calling in the Belgian Special Forces, the Anti-Terrorist Group and overnight plans were made.

★   ★   ★

That morning, a few minutes before the bank opened for business, five different hotel rooms dotted around the square in which the bank was situated were simultaneously raided by a mixed squad of heavily armed men who approached the designated hotels from the rear.

Using a pass key, the door to Room 1 was thrown open to reveal a man by a window assembling a rifle. On seeing the array of weapons pointing his way, the would-be assassin wisely dropped the butt of the rifle he had been holding and threw his hands at the ceiling.

On crashing into Room 2, a squad disturbed a man sleeping peacefully in his bed. When the man opened his eyes to find himself surrounded by pointing guns fitted with silencers, being of a delicate nature, he fell into a faint.

The door of Room 3 opened to expose a man by a window who was fitting a silencer to an already assembled rifle. Instinctively, the man went for the Heckler and Koch pistol on the bedside table and any one of four silenced bullets killed him before he made the reach.

When a squad burst into Room 4, they at first thought they had disturbed a couple in bed, but on pulling back the bedcover, they saw that the wide-eyed, flushed-faced, frightened man was not holding a woman in his arms but a latex-rubber facsimile of one. As the man protectively held the rubber woman, the squad laughed as the joker in the pack stuck the silencer of his automatic pistol into the perfectly shaped, luscious mouth of the doll and said, 'Don't bat an eye or I'll pop your balloon.'

As one member of the squad put it later, there's not a lot of humour in the business, you've got to get your laughs when you can.

The door to Room 5 opened to disclose a man by the window viewing the outside square through a telescopic sight fitted to an already assembled rifle. The man attempted to turn the gun on the invaders and that was the last mistake he ever made.

He was dead before he got halfway round.

The captured terrorist was questioned but, even as taciturn as he was, it quickly became obvious to his interrogators that he was not the one known as Azrael. After questioning, the assassin was gifted to Inspector Javier who charged him with conspiracy to murder. The fact that he was able to list al-Qaeda as co-conspirators delighted him no end.

Three mobile phones were taken on the raids but it would take time and electronic wizards to unlock any secrets they might hold. For now, the possibility was that Azrael was somewhere in the neighbourhood, but even after rechecking every passport held by every hotel in the immediate area, they were no closer to identifying the man they all wanted to see dead.

From there, the police inspector placed two armed, uniformed men on the steps leading up to the bank while the CIA and MOSSAD agents mingled with the crowd in and around the central square.

From then, it became a waiting game with each agent trying to foresee how Jacks would make his approach to the bank. They all knew that he would not be turning up in a dark Ford Focus. After that the possibilities became endless. The most outrageous prediction came from a CIA agent who suggested that Jacks might turn up on a bicycle with Cassandra von Deker riding in tandem.

Who could say with a man like Jacks?

★ ★ ★

Sitting by a window in his hotel room, watching the entrance to the bank through a pair of high-resolution, racing-binoculars, Azrael too was wondering how Mister Jacks would make his approach. Jacks would know that everyone knew he was driving a dark Ford Focus so he would need to find another way of transporting himself to the bank.

Problem was, there were so many ways he could accomplish the feat. But where Azrael did not know how Jacks would make his approach to the bank, he *did* know that he certainly would make one and, when he did, he would be accompanied by Cassandra von Deker.

Azrael did not know exactly what Jacks looked like; he was working on the description supplied by the dead maid, Katrina, and from a blurred photograph lifted from CCTV footage of a man wearing a baseball cap that did more to advertise New York City than it did the man's face.

Azrael would have found it difficult to pick Jacks out of a six-man line-up but he knew Cassandra von Deker's face well enough to pick it out from a crowd. His three long guns positioned round the square had her face imprinted on their minds and when she was spotted so would be the man beside her.

The long guns were instructed only to shoot the woman; he himself would take out Jacks. The havoc Jacks had inflicted over the last hours had shifted him to being a priority target, a man to be killed on sight. But where al-Hashashin and its parent, al-Qaeda, had their reasons for wanting Jacks dead, he planned to kill him for reasons of his own.

Azrael had grown to dislike Mister Jacks as

he had never before disliked any man. Not only had Jacks killed his mentor and nine of his brothers in arms, he had stolen the thunder. With his latest release on the Net receiving over 15,000 hits on opening night, it was he, Azrael, whom everyone should be talking about, but with his exploits in London and at La Capelle it was Jacks who would be nominated for an Oscar.

The only way to reclaim the thunder was to kill Jacks. Do that and the name of Azrael would be on everyone's lips for a long time to come.

Killing him would be a pleasure.

★ ★ ★

Jacks had told Gabriella that Cassandra knew about their overnight liaison and in describing her somewhat jealous reaction, he had asked her to be gentle with the girl. With his request in mind, Gabriella spent the journey to Luxemburg doing exactly that, restricting the conversation to general topics, covering many subjects but never once even coming close to discussing the man up front in the driving seat.

Gabriella felt a certain sympathy for Cassandra in that she knew the girl was way out of her depth with a man like Jacks. At one point last night, he had gone way ahead of herself and she had held on tightly in the fear that he would leave her behind. Last night at dinner, he had described himself as being a savage at heart and he certainly made love like one. She had gone to his bed in order to seduce him, but somewhere in their heated passion he had taken control, from then she had become so wanton the memory excited her.

Seated beside Gabriella, still feeling self-conscious about being dressed as a maid, Cassandra knew she was being gentled along with small talk and flattery and she suspected that Gabriella was aware that she knew about last night so the drive to Luxemburg proved to be seemingly the longest most uncomfortable journey she had ever made. Could any situation be more hurtful than to find herself trapped in a car with the woman who last night had been to bed with the man she loved? And, no matter how Jacks tried to talk her out of it, she did love him. Her dream was that one day he would love her back. She was 21 today with the rest of her life in front of her, plenty of time in which to pursue her dream, assuming, of course, that that life did not suddenly end in Luxemburg.

Earlier that morning, Gabriella used a route-finder on her computer and printed out a route that began close to the château and ended right outside the Luxemburg bank. As Jacks drove, she acted as navigator and during what qualified as the longest car drive of her life, she discovered how difficult it was to converse with the woman who loves the man she had slept with last night. She was therefore somewhat relieved when she told Jacks to take a right, drive by the statue of Charlemagne, and that the bank was at the end of the square.

As Jacks pulled to a stop, the central clock-tower bell was chiming the half-hour.

⋆ ⋆ ⋆

The watching Azrael had a moment's concern when not long ago a police car pulled up outside the bank and dropped off two armed gendarmes who took up positions at the top of the steps. Since their arrival, nothing had happened and he reasoned that perhaps the bank was expecting a large consignment of money or gold. Who knew what was buried in the vaults of a private bank?

As Azrael shifted his binoculars over the sparsely populated square beneath, he saw a cream Rolls Royce glide by. Betting himself a million pounds that it was going to the bank, he followed it all the way there, intrigued by the woman wearing a wide-brimmed hat, whom he caught a glimpse of in the back seat.

When the Rolls parked in a reserved parking space in front of the bank, Azrael watched as the chauffeur got out, carrying no doubt madam's valise in his hand, and did his duty by opening the rear door. The chauffeur's back and open door restricted his view for a moment but he was ready and focused when the woman in the grey hat got out. He had imagined that she would be beautiful and beautiful she certainly was, he thought, as his eyes followed her almost to the top of the bank steps. As he moved the binoculars down, the maid turned her head and, when he saw her in clear profile, he immediately recognized her as Cassandra von Deker and if she was von Deker then the man wearing a chauffeur's uniform who had just disappeared into the bank, had to be Mister Jacks.

In preparation for the big event, Azrael had earlier eaten a larger than usual piece of hashish and where the drug usually height-ened his senses and excitement it was now heightening a bitter sense of defeat and failure. How had Jacks done it, he asked himself? Who was the woman in the hat, and where, in the name of Allah, had he acquired a Rolls Royce? And, more concerning, where were his long guns? If he had spotted Cassandra von Deker then surely at least one of the three men had picked her out. And if one had, then where had been the exploding head? Where was the blood?

Instinctively, Azrael reached for his mobile phone intent on contacting his shooters, but a sudden thought stopped him dead in his tracks. What if his long guns had not shot Cassandra von Deker because they were no longer alive to do so? What if they themselves were dead? Jacks was supposed to be a loner in the field, but what if he had allies, hidden allies that perhaps even he did not know about?

As Azrael's thoughts helter-skeltered round his head his doubts, suspicions and fears came to unite then dragged him off on to the planes of paranoia. Driven by the insidious condition, he decided to get out of there. With such intention in mind, he slipped on his coat, put his Colt Python in a pocket, gathered his papers, money, car keys and his mobile phone then quickly left the hotel room. His car was in a car-park a few streets away and he left fully intending to reach it and then to drive out of Luxemburg as fast as he could, but by the time he reached the outside pavement he was having second thoughts about his intended course of action.

The original contract had been to kill the von Deker woman and Azrael knew al-Qaeda would be angry when they learned that the mission was a failure. They would be angry at him to start with, but they would be even angrier if they learned that he had run away.

As one paranoid, drug-driven fear was replaced by another, by the time Azrael crossed the square, he had decided not to run simply because he could not bring himself to do so. He was the star in the movie of his life. He had cast himself as the ruthless assassin and ruthless assassins do not run. How would he appear to his public if they learned that at the end, Azrael had run away? The only way to give the public the ending they would love was for the ruthless assassin to kill Jacks. Kill Jacks and the thunder would quickly return to where it belonged. And the more he thought on it the more he realized that Jacks would not be that hard to kill.

Azrael knew for certain that Jacks was in the bank; all he had to do was wait until he came out and then kill him. The von Deker woman would most likely stay inside. Her business with Jacks was over. That meant that Jacks would probably be leaving with the woman in the wide-brimmed hat. So, even if he had shed the chauffeur's uniform for another disguise, he would be recognizable by the company he kept.

The more he thought about it, the more Azrael was taken by his plan. He would kill the hated Jacks even if it meant walking right up to him and shooting him at point-blank range. And he would be able to do that. Jacks, like everyone else, had no idea what Azrael looked like and his white skin was still the supreme disguise.

He would walk right up to Jacks, filming as he went and then he would film his face as a bullet tore through him. It would be a masterpiece, not only would Jacks be dead but everyone would at last learn what he looked like.

What a wonderful ending to the film he was already thinking of calling, The Man Who Shot Mister Jacks.

17

When Cassandra, Gabriella and Jacks entered the grand reception area of the bank, a grey-haired man in a dark suit came hurrying towards them. When it became obvious that he was making straight for Gabriella, Cassandra raised a stopping hand and said, 'I am Cassandra von Deker. I believe I am expected.'

'Of course,' the man replied, as he did an immaculate right swerve. 'If you would please follow me.'

As Jacks followed the trio along a richly carpeted corridor hung with portraits of dour-faced men who could only have been bankers, he removed the chauffeur's hat and the jacket. The black trousers were his own and readily matched his black polo-neck sweater. When he finally followed on into a huge room dominated by a table with a top he thought large enough to play football on, he dumped the hat and jacket on the first Louis XIV chair he came across.

Five men were gathered around the table and the one who approached must have been tipped off that the one dressed as a maid was

Cassandra von Deker because he made straight for her. 'Welcome,' he said. 'We are all glad to see you here safely.'

'But perhaps not as glad as we are,' Cassandra responded, in a most aloof manner. Watching, Jacks wondered if she was speaking for the three of them or was using the royal 'we'. 'This is my friend and ally, the Marchioness de Thionville,' she continued turning to Gabriella. 'And this,' she said, turning to Jacks and looking at him with grateful eyes, 'is the man to whom I owe my life. I want him treated with the respect reserved for a knight. Should he even whisper that he would like a glass of water I want one brought quickly to him. Is this understood?'

'It is understood,' the banker replied, as he looked at Jacks who told him he wanted to see his chief security officer. The man was already in the room and, on being summoned, Jacks took him by an arm and led him to a remote corner. 'I want you to take me to an empty room upstairs,' Jacks said, holding the man with steel eyes. 'I need one with a window that overlooks the square. You can do that?'

The security man knew that the man dressed in black had to be the von Deker woman's bodyguard and he was most respectful as he assured Jacks that he knew the ideal room.

'Right,' Jacks responded. 'Just give me a minute,' he concluded, before returning to Cassandra's side, watching a moment as she put her right thumb on a device linked to a computer consol and the consol lit up with a picture of her set underneath her printed name.

'I could have told them who you were,' Jacks said, smiling as Cassandra smiled for him. 'I'm proud of you, kid,' he added, giving her a wink then a kiss on a cheek. 'Don't forget my advice about writing a will. For now, I'm just popping out to post a letter,' he continued, giving her upper right arm an affectionate squeeze. 'But as the man said, I'll be back.' Then, without awaiting a response, but with a telling look at Gabriella, he rejoined the security man who took him to an upstairs room.

Behind him, Jacks left the collection of bankers and lawyers wondering how a mere bodyguard could act so familiarly with one of the richest women in the world and, even more so, they wondered how she could let him be that familiar in public.

As she knew Jacks had been, Cassandra was oblivious to those around her. His show of caring affection, his pride in her was worth more to her than the vast business empire she had just inherited.

She didn't even mind that he had called her kid.

* * *

The room on the second floor of the bank was bare but for another huge table. On entry, Jacks laid his valise on the top and then, causing the security man to raise an eyebrow, he raised his polo-neck sweater to reveal the butt of his Ivor Johnson, extracted it, and then laid it on the table.

'You'll know about Miss von Deker being under threat,' he said, as he unzipped the valise and retrieved the .45, sticking it in his belt where his Ivor Johnson had been. 'Her would-be assassins missed her in London, missed her on the way here,' he went on, as he retrieved his black cashmere coat from the valise, gave it a shake, then slipped it on. 'I was expecting them to be waiting on our arrival, but it looks like our disguise may have fooled them. I'm concerned now that someone on the outside may be waiting for her to come out,' he concluded, as he put the Ivor Johnson in his right coat pocket, retrieved the binoculars from the valise and went to the window that offered a panoramic view of the square.

Standing a little back from the window,

Jacks focused on the first face he saw, and then slowly worked his way round, checking each face as he met it. He spotted a man standing by a newspaper kiosk that he would have bet on being CIA, those Brooks Brothers suits were a giveaway; two sitting at an outside café who were definitely not tourists, but it was only when he got round to the statue of Charlemagne that he saw the face he was searching for. Jacob had been right to describe the cleft chin as definite, it was in the Kirk Douglas class, the thin lips spoke for themselves, his hair was ginger and he had his left hand buried in a coat pocket. If all this was not enough evidence, the man in the dark coat was holding a mobile phone in his right hand and he was aiming it directly at the bank.

The final proof would be to find the ginger-haired man clutching a Colt Python in his pocket.

'Is there a back way out of the bank?' he asked, laying aside the binoculars.

'A side entrance that leads out to the car-park,' the security man answered.

'And from there? Can I get to the back of that statue without having to cross the square?'

'When you come out of the car-park, cross the road and follow the lane facing, keep looking left and you'll see the statue.'

'Right,' Jacks said, gripping his pistol tightly in his coat pocket. 'Take me there; I'll do better scouting the land on the ground.'

When they reached the side entrance, noticing that it was secured by an alarm, Jacks asked the security man to wait here and let him in on return.

'I can do better than that,' the security man said, as he produced a key-ring from a pocket and removed a small Chubb key. 'There are two keys to the door. Use this one; it will automatically deactivate the door alarm.'

'Thanks,' Jacks said sincerely.

'I *would* like it back,' the security man said with a smile.

Jacks grinned in reply, then left the building a man intent on killing the one who called himself Azrael, the self styled Angel of Death. The true Angel of Death had been hovering around Jacks for a long time now and she had yet to claim him.

And she certainly was not going to claim him today.

★ ★ ★

Jacks followed the security man's given route and very quickly the statue on his left came into view. As he drew parallel to it, he slowed his pace until he eventually saw the back of a man wearing a dark coat who was obviously using the plinth of the statue as cover. Without missing a beat, increasing his pace, he turned left and strode directly towards the man, drawing his Ivor Johnson from his coat pocket, pressing it tight against his side as he moved, ready to kill the man if he made the wrong move.

Azrael heard Jacks coming just that second too late. By the time he made to turn for a look, a firm hand was on his left shoulder pulling him back on to something hard that was pressed into the centre of his spine. 'Do exactly as I tell you,' Jacks whispered. 'Or you are dead. Do you understand? Answer me,' he insisted, pushing the Ivor Johnson harder into the man's spine.

'I understand,' Azrael said, in a voice broken by fear.

'You're the one that likes to film people as he kills them aren't you?' Jacks whispered, as he smelt Azrael's fear oozing from his every pore. 'Being tall and skinny with ginger hair, you were probably bullied at school, but that's no excuse for running around killing people. I liked Mr Goldstein. He had a great sense of humour.' As he said the words, he dropped his left hand from Azrael's shoulder and investigated what he was holding in his coat pocket. 'Not a Heckler and Koch,' he said, as he felt the barrel of a gun. 'What are you carrying? I asked you a question,' he concluded with another prod.

'A Colt Python,' Azrael answered.

That was the final proof Jacks needed. 'A big gun for a little man,' he commented.

'You won't shoot me in the back, not a man like you,' Azrael said in false hope.

'You could be right there,' Jacks agreed. 'But then you could be wrong. If you want to find out — just move.'

Azrael stood stock still and, as Jacks heard the tower clock bell wind itself up ready to chime the hour, when the first toll rang out across the square, he was inspired to action. 'Guess what time it is,' he whispered, inciting an answer with another prod from Ivor Johnson.

'It's twelve o'clock,' Azrael answered suspiciously.

'Wrong,' Jacks responded. 'It's High Noon.' And, as he said it, he simultaneously pulled Azrael back by his left shoulder, pressed the Ivor Johnson hard into his spine and pulled the trigger. With the barrel pressed tight against bone, the doctored head of the bullet exploded immediately, shattering Azreal's central vertebrae, sending tiny bone fragments mixed with slivers of copper ripping through his lower lungs and upper stomach, shredding his heart before being absorbed by the inner stomach wall.

As Jacks pulled Azrael backwards, he took the dead weight and lowered it to the ground by the side of the statue, leaving Azrael lying, betraying no sign of his internal injuries. Keeping his head down, he retrieved the dropped mobile phone, stuck it in Azrael's gaping mouth and then folded his hands across his chest.

Jacks left, head down, Ivor Johnson back in his pocket. He was well on his way back to the bank before the clock tower bell tolled the last toll of twelve.

Deed done, it was time now to get out of town.

18

Jacks's allies missed spotting Cassandra von Deker's arrival at the bank. A CIA field agent called Black, seated at an outside café on the square, still waiting patiently to see how Jacks would arrive, swept his eyes around the square, then did a double take as a man taking photographs by the statue of Charlemagne suddenly fell backwards and disappeared from view. Black thought he saw someone behind the man with the camera, but uncertain and very curious he went to investigate. His partner across the way saw him move and Black signalled to him to follow on.

On reaching the statue, the two agents found the body, and with a mobile phone stuck in its mouth and the butt of a Colt Python sticking out of a pocket, it took them not two seconds to identify it as Azrael. 'It's got to be him,' Black said, as he retrieved the mobile and slipped it into a pocket.

'But who?' Field Agent Fleming asked.

'Who do you think?' Black questioned, as he used his own mobile to summon the police.

'Mister Jacks?'

'Who else?' Black responded with a respectful nod of his head.

★ ★ ★

Initially, Inspector Javier was none too pleased to learn that there was another dead body on his doorstep. When he learned from his new made friends in the CIA that the dead man had been an international terrorist-assassin who was listed very high on the FBI's Most Wanted list, he became much more receptive. On being told that he would be mentioned by name in reports, he veritably beamed. He had a friend on the Paris Sûreté who was fond of referring to his contact in the CIA; at long last, he would be able to out boast him.

Azrael's body was taken to the morgue and, as a pathologist checked it over two policemen tracked down his hotel room from which they retrieved a laptop that proved to have a very informative memory bank.

At first, the police assumed that Azrael's British passport was a forgery, but on checking with the Passport Office back in England the passport proved to be genuine.

Upon investigation, Azrael turned out to be from a wealthy background, public school educated. While studying the Art of Film Making at a specialist college, he had become involved with Muslim factions and converted to the faith of Islam. During this period, he gathered four police convictions, two for the possession of cannabis and two for a breach of the peace while taking part in pro-Muslim demonstrations. From such student beginnings, he had somehow gone on to be al-Hashashin's top assassin.

How he had climbed such a ladder was a mystery, but it was agreed by one and all that Azrael was a killer long before he was enlisted into al-Hashashin.

He enjoyed his killing too much to be a man who had merely been trained to kill.

* * *

When Jacks returned to the bank, he found the security man waiting for him at the top of the stairs, valise in hand. As he handed it to Jacks, he said, 'Your binoculars are inside.'

As Jacks handed him the Chubb key, he grinned and said, 'I didn't have time to get a copy cut.'

The security man responded with a smile, and then told Jacks that the ladies were awaiting him.

He led Jacks part way along a corridor then

left him by a door. When Jacks opened it, he walked into an opulent room where Cassandra and Gabriella sat drinking coffee. As he approached, both women laid cups aside then stood up, each betraying a concerned look.

'Don't look so anxious,' he said on approach. 'I only popped out to post a letter, but any minute now someone's going to figure out that it was me who posted it. And when they do, I don't want to be here,' he concluded, before turning to Gabriella and taking her by an arm. As he led her to the door, he said. 'The key is in the ignition. You drive. As soon as you see me coming out of the bank, start the engine. This is a getaway.'

'God,' Gabriella sighed, her face aglow, eyes bright. 'With you it is all so exciting.' Then, with a farewell wave to Cassandra, she left the room to find herself eventually parked outside a bank waiting for her lover to emerge before making their escape. A clichéd scene perhaps. What made this different, she thought with a smile, was that it was to be accomplished in a 1955 classic Silver Cloud Rolls Royce.

⋆　⋆　⋆

With Gabriella gone, Jacks returned to a Cassandra who had about her a look of sadness. 'Must you go?' she asked.

'I must,' Jacks emphasized. 'I really must. So, how do I reach you?'

'You want to see me again?' Cassandra questioned in delight.

'I want to see the woman you've become,' Jacks answered. 'So? How do I reach you?'

Having prepared in hope for such a request, in response, Cassandra extracted a folded piece of paper from the pocket of the maid's uniform she still wore and handed it to Jacks. 'The number can be rung at any time; the door of the address will always be open to you,' she said, looking lovingly at Jacks. 'I shall be there at least until Christmas; it would make me very happy if I were to see you by then.'

'I like an optimist,' Jacks said, smiling, as he accepted the already prepared information and tucked it away inside his coat, then retrieved the .45 and handed it to Cassandra. 'Happy Birthday,' he said, kissing her briefly on her ready to give lips.

How Cassandra flushed and smiled. 'Only you could give a woman a .45 for her birthday.'

'It'll remind you of the night you stood on a public convenience toilet seat ready to shoot the wrong man through the door,' Jacks said, as he looked into her wonderfully alive green eyes. 'Did I tell you how much I admire your courage? All I had to be was my fearless self; you had to be brave. You kept up with me all the way, and there aren't many who could do that.'

'I love you, Mister Jacks,' Cassandra responded, because at that moment, looking into eyes that were now so gentle, her heart went out to him and, as it went, she knew that she had lost it forever.

'My name's Billy Jacks,' he corrected, as he raised Cassandra's right hand to his mouth and kissed it.

'Billy,' Cassandra said softly.

'That's me,' Jacks responded, giving her hand a squeeze before letting go of it. 'It's probably him you love. I try to leave him behind when I'm working, but I'm sure he tags along . . . You'll be all right without me?'

'Not really,' Cassandra said, with a small smile. 'But if you mean will I be *all right*, of course I will be. Not only am I a woman now, I'm a woman with a billion in the bank,' she added, smiling wider.

Jacks smiled just as wide. 'Don't be spending it all at once,' he advised, giving her arm a farewell squeeze. 'Take care. See you then,' he concluded, before turning away and leaving the room without a backward glance.

Where the day had begun with Cassandra

not knowing whether it would end with death, she now stood a woman thinking that this was the most wonderful day of her life. She knew that Billy Jacks was galloping off into the sunset with the beautiful Gabriella but she felt no jealousy. What did she have to envy? Billy did not love Gabriella, but, one day, he would come to love her.

She would never forget her twenty-first birthday. She would remember every moment of the previous forty-eight hours for the rest of her life.

She would remember simply because what had happened to her qualified as being unforgettable.

★　★　★

Later that afternoon when the security man heard the story about what had happened in the square, he quickly put things together. The timing was exact, which meant that Cassandra von Deker's bodyguard left the bank, returned ten minutes later, having killed a man in between. Reports said the dead man was a dangerous terrorist but it was not the fact that the bodyguard had killed him that alarmed the security man, what alarmed him was that he had seen the man no more than minutes after the event and there had been nothing there to betray the fact. The bodyguard had made a joke about not having had time to get a copy of the key cut and he had been smiling.

The security guard was known for his discretion and fully intended keeping his knowledge to himself. Any thought he might have had of telling the authorities would have ultimately been stopped by the thought that to do so could result in the bodyguard finding out.

And who in their right mind would risk making an enemy of such a man?

★　★　★

The CIA told the local police inspector enough to keep him happy, but they did not mention Azrael's mobile phone that later proved a mine of information, containing a full list of everyone Azrael had ever killed, complete with a photograph of each victim and a detailed description of their deaths.

With permission from Inspector Javier, the CIA photographed the dead Azrael in a death pose then arranged for him to be given no special mention in reports. Azrael was just one of three unknown men who had been killed during a major anti-terrorist operation. Azrael was buried anonymously and his parents back in England never did learn of their son's ignominious ending.

When they were done with the police, the CIA men retired to a hotel room and sent a report back to Langley. On receipt of the photograph of the dead Azrael, mobile phone in his mouth, Colt Python clasped across his chest, they arranged for it to be published on the same website that Azrael had used to broadcast his killings.

It was posted under the title The Death of Azrael.

When Langley was taken care of, Agents Black and Fleming used their mobiles to pass on the news, complete with picture, to every fellow field agent on their number list with the request that they send it on to everyone on theirs. Within a couple of hours, there was not a CIA field agent in the world who did not know that Mister Jacks was the man who had taken out Azrael.

When they had done what they came to do, the two agents went downstairs to the bar. Black ordered a double Jack Daniels on the rocks, Fleming had a double Scotch as it came and when their drinks were served, with the sun now shining outside, they carried them out to a table that sat on a balcony overlooking the square where it had all begun.

Although the two men were certain enough that Jacks had done the job on Azrael, they were no further forward in figuring out how he had managed the feat. 'I watched the bank all morning,' Fleming said. 'And I never even saw a couple of any description go into the bank.'

'Neither did I,' Black said. As he said the words, he glanced at the bank under discussion and, as he glanced, he thought something was missing from the picture. When he realized what that something missing was, he as good as got it all at once. 'What's missing from outside the bank?' he asked.

Fleming glanced down. 'The cream Rolls Royce,' he answered.

'That's how Jacks did it,' Black explained. 'We never saw a couple arrive at the bank because he arrived in a threesome. He came as the chauffeur, von Deker as the maid. The woman in the hat had to come with the Rolls Royce. Probably an ally of Jacks's from the past.'

'It fits,' Fleming agreed. 'We missed spotting von Deker, does that mean the enemy did?'

'No, somebody spotted her. Probably Azrael, otherwise he'd still be sitting in his hotel room waiting like we were waiting,'

Black reasoned. 'That's probably when he learnt that his three shooters were no longer by their posts. He spots the woman, figures Jacks as the chauffeur and comes down to the square to wait for him to come out of the bank.'

'Sounds about right,' Fleming agreed. 'So, what's Jacks up to?'

'Jacks makes it into the bank,' Black said, reading the situation as he went along. 'He makes it safe, but he doesn't know if this is because of his clever disguise or because his friends on the ground have taken out the shooters. So, favouring the first, he finds an upstairs window and checks out the square below and while looking for the enemy he spots Azrael.'

'This is where your reasoning falls down,' Fleming said. 'How did Jacks know what Azrael looked like? Even we didn't know he was white.'

'Perhaps Jacks has better intelligence than us,' Black offered. 'Don't forget, he was working for the Fox. It doesn't really matter how Jacks recognized Azrael. He did, and in so doing, he left the bank and killed him.'

'Dressed as a chauffeur?' Fleming questioned doubtfully.

'The chauffeur was carrying a valise,' Black reminded. 'Jacks probably came prepared.

Changed clothes inside the bank then slipped out a back door to get behind Azrael.'

'And then whacked him cold,' Fleming said respectfully. 'Azrael went down without seeing the face of the man who had just killed him. Come the end, Jacks beat him at his own game.'

'And there's more,' Black went on, leaning closer across the table. 'When we were crossing the square to check things out, I remember the church clock was ringing out twelve o'clock.'

'So?' Fleming questioned.

'High Noon,' Black breathed.

Fleming took a moment to take in the full portent of what Black had said. When he had captured it all, he sat back in his seat. 'Wow!' he exclaimed, in a whisper. 'And I haven't used that expression since I was a kid back in Ohio. Wow! Wow! Wow!' he intoned admiringly. 'He's *good* Jacks, isn't he?'

'He's the best I never saw,' Black stated.

19

As always, on successfully completing a mission, Jacks was feeling somewhat empty, somewhat drained. It had been a couple of days to remember, but he figured that even he could not live at that pace for too long and he consoled himself with the knowledge that where the excitement and danger revolving round death had come and passed, the excitement of life was still there to be savoured.

With such thoughts, he turned his eyes on Gabriella, rich dark hair now hanging free, that marvellous profile of hers, an intent look on her face as she steered the Rolls through the countryside.

Gabriella had not said anything since they drove away from the bank and thinking that his own silence was the cause of hers, he broke the mood by smiling her way and saying, 'After what we've been through, don't you think it's time you knew my name?'

Relieved that the distant man had come back to her, Gabriella smiled in turn. 'It's not Mister Jacks?' she asked, in mock surprise.

'Only when I'm working,' Jacks replied. 'In

213

between, I'm known as Billy Jacks.'

'Billy Jacks,' Gabriella enunciated. 'It has a certain ring to it.'

'That's probably because it's not the name I was born to,' Jacks responded. 'It's a name I earned on the streets of South London.'

'How did you earn it,' Gabriella asked, as she glided the car round a large sweeping bend. 'How does one earn a name?'

'It's not easy,' Jacks answered. 'I earned mine in a card game. Do you know stud-poker?'

'One card down, four cards up,' Gabriella replied. 'And I didn't learn the game from my husband; I learned it from my father. He loved to gamble.'

'So do I,' Jacks stated. 'The way I live, my whole life is a gamble . . . So, there I was sitting at my favourite table playing my favourite game when I was dealt the kind of hand you dream about. The kind that can't lose. As you'll know, having a good hand isn't enough; to make it pay the other players need to have good hands and that night, I had three good hands to bet into. Two were bet out of the game and that left me facing two aces and two queens with it being pretty certain that the hole card made it a full house. I was sitting with three jacks showing and one in the hole. At the last call, I bet big

214

and the full house didn't have enough to cover the bet. He was so sure that he had me; he put his Omega watch into the pot and called. You should have seen his face when I turned over the fourth jack. As I raked in the winnings, someone at the table said, 'Four Jacks Billy' and another, a quite notorious character, improved on that by saying Billy Jacks. I've been him ever since and I still wear the watch. Every time I look at it, I'm reminded of that night.'

'So you were christened at a poker table,' Gabriella mused, with a smile. 'What an auspicious start to life.'

'Dubbed by a bank robber in a den of iniquity,' Jacks said with a chuckle.

Gabriella responded in kind and then asked, 'Did you tell Cassandra your name was Billy?'

'Of course I did,' Jacks replied. 'But I was in too much of a hurry to tell her the story . . . That reminds me, I never asked her if she wrote a will. Did she?'

'She took your advice,' Gabriella answered. 'I signed the document as a witness.'

'Who did she leave it all to?'

'At first she thought of just signing Deker Industries over to you,' Gabriella answered. 'But she decided that she didn't want to spoil you by leaving you all those guns to play with.'

'She said that?' Jacks questioned with a laugh.

'She did,' Gabriella confirmed. 'But she had already made up her mind. In the event of her untimely, suspicious death fifty per cent goes to the Red Cross and fifty per cent goes to the Red Crescent. For now, she has donated a large sum to both services with a guarantee of the same amount when she has finished dismantling her arms industry.'

'She's going to close Deker Industries?' Jacks questioned in delighted surprise.

'Not entirely,' Gabriella answered. 'Deker Industries is also involved in the making of farm machinery. Cassandra is going to shift her resources and make more tractors that can be exported cheaply to the Third World . . . I didn't personally know Cassandra before our encounter but I knew her by reputation. And it would need to be said that you have been a great influence on her. She's certainly changed her ways.'

'It wasn't me who changed her,' Jacks said in denial, 'it was her experiences. Perhaps knowing that men were trying to kill her with guns supplied by Deker Industries was the influence,' he suggested. 'Or standing on a toilet seat with a .45 in her hand ready to shoot the bad guys. Put it all together and it's not really surprising that she's come out of it with a different attitude to life. But it had nothing to do with me.'

Gabriella smiled and shook her head at the man she loved. 'You won't take responsibility for anything, will you?' she stated, as much as asked.

'Not if I can duck,' Jacks answered, smiling back. 'I don't mind being responsible for peoples' lives, but don't ask me to be responsible for the in betweens, I'm not qualified to take care of feelings and emotions.'

'And you're not just talking about Cassandra, are you?' Gabriella remarked sagely. 'You're telling me personally. Fortunately, you haven't told me anything I didn't already know or suspect . . . You do know that Cassandra is in love with you?'

'As I seem to be saying a lot these days,' Jacks replied, a bit shortly, 'I don't know what it means to be in love. But, where I've never met love,' he went on, reaching over with his left hand to squeeze the top of Gabriella's thigh through her thin dress, 'fortunately I am familiar with her incitative sisters, lust, passion and desire.' As Gabriella dropped a hand from the steering wheel on to his and moved it further up her thigh, he continued, 'I like them; they're my kind of people.'

'God,' Gabriella breathed. 'You make me feel so wanton. I am wet at your touch,' she sighed, squeezing her eyes shut.

'Keep your eyes on the road,' Jacks said in mock reproof, smiling as he removed his hand. 'I don't want this to end like *The Wages of Fear*.'

'It won't,' Gabriella responded in a somewhat husky tone. 'I have a much happier ending in mind.'

'Wonderful,' Jacks said sincerely, as he read the promise in Gabriella's eyes. 'I love a happy ending; it's a great beginning to whatever might follow. But it's not all over yet,' he continued. 'When we get to the château, I have a phone call to make. After that, you're all mine and I'm all yours. In the meantime, control your animal urges.'

Gabriella laughed and, as she did so, she recalled how she and Charles had never shared laughter. Charles had no sense of humour and where she had laughed in the company of others, she had never laughed when alone with him. Billy Jacks even brought humour into bed with him; last night they had shared laughter when, in their excitement, he banged his head on the oak headboard; she could not imagine Charles finding humour in such a situation. Like all Frenchmen, Charles thought lovemaking was a serious business.

After Charles, she had thought never to

love again nor had she wanted to. Charles the Marquis and Billy Jacks began by being dangerous men, but the similarity ended there. After that, the man seated beside her was so different from Charles as to be from another species.

As she neared the château, Gabriella resolved never to truly tell Billy Jacks how she felt about him. It was better that she just lusted after him; to love him would be to risk losing him and he was a man she never wanted to lose. She was wise enough to know that the time would come when he would move on from the château but she did not care how often he left her, so long as he always came back.

When he did, he would find her waiting.

★   ★   ★

On arrival, Gabriella found a somewhat relieved, anxious butler awaiting her. When Jacks went upstairs to freshen up and make his phone call, Ronald asked if he could have a word, then led the way into the kitchen area where a television was broadcasting a news bulletin.

Gabriella immediately recognized the pictures of the Luxemburg square showing the bank from which she had only so recently driven away. As she listened to the report of an anti-terrorist raid, linked to the one the night before at La Capelle, her mind raced as she tried to take it all in. When she had heard enough, she made a decision.

'I want you to do something for me, Ronald,' she asked, as she switched off the television. 'I want you to forget you know this. I never want you to mention it to me, and I would ask you please never to mention it to my guest. Will you do this for me?'

Ronald nodded. 'I understand, madam.'

'Thank you, Ronald,' Gabriella said sincerely. 'Over the years, you have become my friend as well as the man who takes care of my life.'

Ronald smiled. 'Then, as your friend,' he responded, 'I feel the need to warn you that your guest is dangerous, dangerous in a different way.'

'I know,' she confessed. 'Perhaps that's his appeal. But you musn't concern yourself about me, Ronald. According to Cassandra von Deker, I'm the most sophisticated woman she's ever met. So what do I have to be concerned about?' she asked. 'I just hope you have something nice on the stove. I'm hungry and if I'm hungry then it's certain that my guest will be starving. He has such a hunger.'

'I'm sure he has, madam,' Ronald said diplomatically.

Ronald had been there for madam on the death of her husband and, as he watched Gabriella leave the kitchen, he consoled himself with the thought that if tragedy was to strike her down then he would be there again, ready with a shoulder for her to cry on.

* * *

As Gabriella climbed the stairs to her bedroom, she mused over what she had learned from the television. According to the news, three terrorists had been killed and one taken into custody. The timing was right, but Mister Jacks was only gone from the bank a mere fifteen minutes at the outside. Was it possible to kill three men in such a short time? What did not make it right was that one terrorist had been taken alive and Mister Jacks didn't strike her as a man who took prisoners. But the timing was so exact, so Gabriella concluded by thinking that what-ever had happened, Mister Jacks was in there somewhere.

Unless Jacks chose to tell her, Gabriella accepted that she would never know what happened in that quarter of an hour he was absent from the bank because she certainly

221

would never ask him.

Not ever.

Gabriella's thoughts on the matter ended with a smile as she realized that never again could she hear someone say they were just popping out to post a letter without their words taking on a whole new meaning.

As Gabriella entered her bedroom and began to undress for a shower, she felt that tell-tale tightening in her groin. How she ached for him; how she longed again to feel him inside her, filling her up. Charles the Marquis always made love as a gentleman, in that he gave more than he took. Billy Jacks was more the savage; he took more than he gave. But, as he could give her more than enough, then she was happy for him to take from her as much as he needed. That was how she would love him, that was how she would keep him ever coming back for more. She would feed his needs as no other woman ever had and no other woman ever could.

She would be his Mistress Immaculate.

★   ★   ★

When Jacks had showered and dressed, he lay on the bed and made a phone call that he knew would prove very interesting. On receiving a reply, he said, 'This is Billy.'

'Billy,' Jacob echoed. 'How good it is to hear from you again. You are safe?'

'Safe enough,' Jacks replied. 'So, how did I do?' he questioned. 'I know I delivered the package safely; I'm talking about the other side of things.'

'The other side of things?' Jacob questioned.

'Come on, you old fox,' Jacks challenged. 'It was pretty obvious from the start that any of the major players could have airlifted Cassandra in and out of Luxemburg in a couple of hours. What was it? Did the CIA not want to show their hand to al-Qaeda, or was it just that you had a better idea? You knew al-Hashashin were the hitters in Kensington; you knew I had hit two of them previously, and you reckoned that once they heard I was running the package that they would read me as being no more than a hired bodyguard, then come after me with a vengeance. You were right, they did. You used Cassandra as bait for the crows and as I mowed you reaped. So tell me, how did I do? Was it a good harvest?'

'It wasn't quite so cold-blooded as that,' Jacob claimed. 'I began by knowing that you were the man to see Cassandra safely to Luxemburg. And I was right there.'

'Fair enough,' Jacks accepted. 'But, after that?'

'I did think that you might draw out the

enemy,' Jacob conceded. 'And your doing so yielded a far greater crop than expected or hoped for,' he went on. 'The computer found at the garage finally led to a raid on a house in Watford. What was found there led to a further three raids on premises, one of which proved to be a bomb-making factory. The French did just as well. The houses they raided in Paris and Marseilles led to other raids and the location of al-Qaeda bases in Spain and Germany. It's been a very busy night for the security services, it could be said that you brought down al-Qaeda's entire European network.'

'It could be said perhaps,' Jacks agreed. 'But it would be a lie. All I did was kill some bad guys who were intent on killing me and Cassandra. I kicked things off, security agencies shut things down but, in between, it was the machine that brought down the al-Qaeda network. They were betrayed by their servants, the mobile phone, the laptop and the PC. You have to watch machines, Jacob, they have no souls. They'll tear your arm off without an apology then betray you without a blush.'

'A wise warning,' Jacob said. 'And I hope the fact that I misused you does not affect our friendship.'

'You're a devious, manipulative, ruthless

man, Jacob,' Jacks responded. 'And that's three good reasons for me liking you.'

Jacob chuckled. 'It's good to hear you know me so well. I value our relationship, I would hate for it to falter on the rocks.'

'I doubt it ever will,' Jacks said. 'The way I see it, you asked me to do you a service; I did you that service. After that, the side benefits are all yours. I have my own rewards to claim . . . and talking of doing a service, I'd like you to do me a favour.'

'Just ask,' Jacob said.

'Have you got a pen and paper handy?' Jacks began. 'Take down this name and address . . . She's a lone parent with a little girl and a ginger tom-cat called Rambo living in a one-bedroom council flat. I want you to arrange that she gets relocated to a three-bedroom house in a nicer location close to a better school.'

'It will be done,' Jacob promised.

'Once she the kid and the cat have moved,' Jacks continued, 'I want you to arrange for her to win some big prize, not too much, I don't want to frighten her. Let's say a quarter of a million sterling. And I want the prize delivered to her by someone gentle who will take care of the bank for her and who perhaps could advise her on what best to do with the money.'

'I know just the man,' Jacob responded. 'You certainly have a way with you, Billy,' he granted. 'Never have I known you to ask a favour for yourself.'

'This is a girl who genuinely believes she was born unlucky,' Jacks explained. 'When next I see her, I want to find a girl faced with the reality that her luck has changed. Actually, I'm doing myself a favour, pessimists are hard work. Next time I see her, I won't have to spend half the night trying to cheer her up. Just one more thing . . . '

'Yes?' Jacob questioned.

'When you've memorized the address, swallow the evidence,' Jacks instructed with a grin.

Jacob chuckled down the phone. 'That sense of humour of yours never deserts you, does it?'

'If it ever does,' Jacks claimed, 'then I'm a dead man. My sense of humour is my first line of defence against the harsh realities of my existence. The secret is not to wait six months to see the funny side, see the funny side now, and from where I stand, there always is a funny side to be seen . . . Anyway, Jacob, I have to go. As I said, I have my own crop to gather, a harvest of beauty, charm and grace. I don't know when I'll be back in London. In the meantime, unless it's a case of

Nicole Kidman being kidnapped, don't ring me tomorrow.'

'I won't, but I probably will ring you in the future.'

'By then,' Jacks said, 'I'll probably be glad to hear from you. See you then,' he concluded, then switched off the mobile.

When Jacks went downstairs to meet the waiting Gabriella his nostrils were tantalized by something tasty being cooked somewhere in the château. He had not eaten since early that morning and the smell in the air set his palate tingling and his stomach rumbling. He had more than one hunger waiting to be fed but, for now, what he needed more than anything was something to eat.

He was starving.

EPILOGUE

Osama bin Laden, [CIA codename — The Contractor] had passed the reins of al-Qaeda [Arabic for The Base] on to his eldest son, Saad bin Laden, [CIA codename — The Broker] but where the son ran field operations, the father remained the power behind the throne and two days after the débâcle in Europe, he called a council meeting to which he summoned his closest advisers.

The Council Meeting was held in a heavily guarded compound situated in Khowst, a mountainous region in the Pakati Province of Eastern Afghanistan and it was attended by Saif el-Adel, al-Qaeda's Chief of Military Operations and head of al-Hashashin; Mullah Mohammed Omar, the leader of the Taliban and by Abullah Ahmed Abdullah, al-Qaeda's chief financial adviser.

Saif el-Adel had fought beside Osama bin Laden in the Mujihadin — The Holy Warriors — in the war against the Soviet infidel invaders; he had been with him in 1988 when he founded al-Qaeda and turned the war into a Jihad against the West but, even though he was a life-long friend of the man sitting beside a Kalashnikov, when he was called upon to explain what had happened to so disrupt their European network, he did so hoping that he would be forgiven his great failure.

El-Adel did not shrink from accepting full responsibility for the disaster; he spelt it out, bullet by bullet, and when he had bared his soul in shame he turned the subject round to one of revenge. 'Do we kill the woman?' he asked.

Osama bin Laden shook his head. 'No,' he replied. 'She was never our enemy; she was but a means to an end. Is it true that she is closing down the arms side of Deker Industries to concentrate on the making of farm machinery?'

'So it has been reported in the Western press,' el-Adel answered.

'Interesting,' bin Laden mused. 'Another reason for not killing her is that her bodyguard earned her life. Like us, this Mister Jacks is a warrior. We are united in faith and in cause; our war is a crusade. This Mister Jacks is a lone warrior, outcast in faith, with no cause; he fights his own war. He is a man we should respect but even in respect he must forfeit his life.'

'A man like him is certain to resurface,'

el-Adel pointed out.

'This is true,' bin Laden agreed. 'But we must not wait until he does so. We must begin now to hunt him down. Let the name Mister Jacks be known to all our people. Let it be known that the man who kills him will be rewarded with Paradise on earth, all he desires, all he wills, shall be his.'

'So shall it be,' el-Adel swore.

We do hope that you have enjoyed reading this large print book.

Did you know that all of our titles are available for purchase?

We publish a wide range of high quality large print books including:
Romances, Mysteries, Classics
General Fiction
Non Fiction and Westerns

Special interest titles available in large print are:
The Little Oxford Dictionary
Music Book
Song Book
Hymn Book
Service Book

Also available from us courtesy of Oxford University Press:
Young Readers' Dictionary
(large print edition)
Young Readers' Thesaurus
(large print edition)

For further information or a free brochure, please contact us at:
Ulverscroft Large Print Books Ltd.,
The Green, Bradgate Road, Anstey,
Leicester, LE7 7FU, England.
Tel: (00 44) **0116 236 4325**
Fax: (00 44) **0116 234 0205**

Other titles published by
The House of Ulverscroft:

BAVARIAN SUNSET

James Pattinson

Sam Grant had to trace the vendor of a painting that had come up for sale at a London auction room. By a German Jewish artist who had perished in a Nazi concentration camp, the painting had been stolen from a schloss in Lower Saxony in World War Two. Then it had apparently vanished, until surfacing fifty years later. So who had possessed it in those years? Grant had to find the answer for Gerda Hoffman, an attractive blonde. But the case turned out to have a fatal aspect.